Brother Dale

The energy and
vibe you bring
to the world is ama
and will now be multipli
in your golf game and
world betterment. May your
every breath bring you
closer to enlightenment.

Love and Tujechey,

Praise for *Tantric Golf and Buddha Fields*

"In golf, life, or business, aligning your spirit is essential if you want to achieve your goals. *Tantric Golf* will help you to shed your illusions and find the fairway, in golf and life." **-- David Meltzer,** CEO of Sports 1 Marketing and International Best-Selling Author

"*Tantric Golf* combined the funny lines of *Caddyshack,* the intense gambling of *Rounders*, and the spiritual teachings of the *Little Buddha* all in one relatable book! I loved it! **-Tralain Benner,** CEO Mama T's Pet Products

"Kevin and Daniel masterfully highlight the ancient spiritual traditions of Buddhism through captivating storytelling. For those seeking to open their mind and live a life free of anger, jealousy, and internal suffering Tantric Golf teaches and shows you through the simple day to day practices how you can transform and bring peace to yourself and those around you. Great job!" -**David Braaten,** *CEO & COO* **Partnership Bank**

"A spiritual journey into the mind, body, and soul. Captivating and inspiring, this book will improve your outlook on life, golf, and one's own existence. Thanks for sharing such a personal quest!"-**John Lepak,** Golfing and Teaching Professional.

"**The Three Priceless Techniques** changed my game!"-**Steve Martin**, CFO FilterSteve.com

"Let me start by saying *Tantric Golf* was an absolute joy to read. It was beautifully crafted, and the words rolled off the page. I thoroughly enjoyed the "golf talk" dialogue. You know instantly upon reading that a seasoned lifelong golfer had to have written this book. It was part of the fun of the read. Authenticity was a key element of this book, but the very purpose of the book was at first a bit tough for me to swallow.

Truth be told, I am a skeptic by nature. I am reticent to accept anything that smacks of an alternative way of being. For me, the path to success is good old fashion time and physical grit. I guess you can say I live in a material world; there ain't a lot of Zen circulating around within me!

However, I always knew there was something terribly missing from my golf game. I am a relatively solid ball striker, and I'm quite the athlete on the range. Yet when I walk to the first tee, I soon discover that when I look up every fairway is lined with treachery and demons. Among my golf buddies, I am famous for failing to look up and taking aim. But this is not because I neglected to develop this important golf habit. Rather I am too terrified to look up knowing that all I will see is the raging inferno of hell burning before me. That's the truth. I needed help.

Tantric Golf helped teach me there was another way to golf.... and another way to see. Bravo! Thank you, Kevin and Daniel."-**Howard G. Maron MD,** Former Doctor for the Seattle Supersonics and Portland Trailblazers, Founder MD^2

"Tantric Golf is a MUST BUY BOOK! It is a roadmap to success in golf and fulfillment in life. Incredibly relatable, fun, funny and shared "tour tips" and golf secrets"-**Scott Johnson,** 1996 NCAA Team Champion, Arizona St. University, 1997 GCAA and Academic First Team All American, Pac 12 First Team, Pac 12 Champion, and Dave Williams Award Winner

"Daniel's incredible new book took me through the passage of spirituality and soul in a manner I never knew before. An inspiration into self-awareness and enlightenment. Thank you for the experience and the possibilities."-**Sassan Sobhani,** CEO ai SECURITY LLC

"Intriguing book to read from start to finish. Daniel has done a masterful job of describing how through using some simple techniques life changing events could occur. He inspires us to become more aware of our own behavior, our environment, and people around us." **-Dr. Jalal Alisobhani,** CEO of Acculink

"Tantric Golf reveals the **Three Priceless Techniques** that will help you win not only in the Game of Golf but also in the Game of Life! The story contains effective Buddhist and spiritual principles that can help improve your gamesmanship in all aspects of your life. This book will give you the winning edge in living joyfully!"-**Robert K.J. Wu,** *Author of So Now So Tao: a Taoist Approach to Harmonic Wealth*

"**The Three Priceless Techniques** in Daniel's new book are transformative treasures indeed, as well as wise, accessible and practical—and I use them myself. I delight in what he has done here with his spiritual parable, a perfect fit for our time, place, and troubled world, and recommend it heartily to all those who seek a better life and world for us all."**-Lama Surya Das,** author of *Awakening the Buddha Within; Tibetan Wisdom for the Western World,* Founder of the Dzogchen Meditation Center.

"This book is an inspiring and delightful tool for daily practices. It teaches simple techniques that today's humanity needs to deal with their day-to-day challenges. It is also a great beginning to understand suffering and connect with your inner Buddha."**-Sri Madhuji**

"Daniel, what a phenomenal book! I so enjoyed the story and the teachings. **The Three Priceless Techniques** that you describe (and show how to use in our everyday lives) are so powerful that I am incorporating them into my own practice. What a gift you have written for humanity, as it will change how people look at themselves and the world. You will know you are different and transformed from the minute you wake up in the morning. Thank you, thank you!!!" **-Dr. Eric Robins**, co-author of *Your Hands Can Heal You*

"Daniel O'Hara brings joy, inspiration, and uniqueness to this spiritual journey of wisdom that will touch, heal and uplift the young and old alike. A must read!"-**Kim Somers Egelsee,** #1 best-selling author of *Getting Your Life to a 10+*

"Daniel's *Buddha Fields* is such a relatable story. An investment of an hour will pay dividends for the rest of your life!"-**Loren Slocum, CEO** of Lobella Int'l and author of *Life Tune-ups: Your Personal Plan to Find Balance, Discover Your Passion, and Step into Greatness*

"Daniel has written an "old soul" book. It's full of ancient wisdom, but it's exceptionally applicable in the modern world. It's evolved, practical and easy-to-use."-**John Merryman,** co-author of *Your Hands Can Heal You*

"There's a volcano's worth of energy, power, light, and transformation inside this little book!"-**Karen Rauch Carter,** author of *Move Your Stuff, Change Your Life* and *Make a Shift, Change Your Life*

"Daniel O'Hara brings practical Buddhism to daily life in his new book, *Buddha Fields.* In simple parable form, he teaches us how to improve our lives and the lives of those around us without excessive words and practices. Daniel is a master spiritual teacher of the obscured by gently and effectively opening our eyes to the obvious. A great read for anyone and everyone." **-Tom Zender,** President Emeritus of Unity Church

Tantric Golf™

Buddha Fields for Golfers

By

Kevin PomArleau and

Daniel O'Hara

This book and other titles and videos can be found at:

www.TantricGolf.com

Printed in the U.S.A

The purpose of this book is to help you, the reader, find your *Buddha Fairway,* to make a few more putts, to live a better life, to laugh, and most importantly, to get out of suffering. Buddhist or not, this book is for everyone.

We hope that you enjoy these most relatable life stories, practical golf tips, and more importantly, learn how to utilize and apply the **THREE PRICELESS TECHNIQUES.** These **Techniques** will help you find your *Buddha Fairway* in life, while mentally keeping you out of the deep rough, and effortlessly freeing you of limiting beliefs and negative thoughts.

The story below is inspired by the real events of a golfer who was in search of the dream life--playing golf on the PGA and Champions Tours--only to find himself in the deep rough, time after time, until being introduced to the **THREE PRICELESS TECHNIQUES**.

This dramatic and at times humorous novel, depicting the journey of a golfer finding his *Buddha Fairway* in life, will inspire you... Enjoy!

“Of all the hazards, fear is the worst.”- **Slammin’ Sammy Snead**

“The mind messes up more shots than the body.”

- Tommy Bolt

“To be consistently effective, you must put a certain distance between yourself and what happens to you on the golf course. This is not indifference, it's detachment.”

- Slammin’ Sammy Snead

Table of Contents

The Gamble

What a relief to have the excessively tight handcuffs removed before I being shoved thru the steel entry-way. "BANG!" The steel cell door slammed shut behind me. The sound of the bolt sliding into the lock-hole was like fingernails across a chalkboard jolting me to the core.

As I looked around the cell, I spotted an empty place to sit in the corner of the cold grungy floor. It was obvious that law enforcement was having a pretty lucrative night, as I weaved around all of the sleeping bodies on the floor. "Excuse me," I said, as I leaned into the wall and slid to the ground. My brain is pounding against the inside of my skull as if I had just gone 12 rounds with "Iron" Mike Tyson.

I attempted to look around without making eye contact and realized that my arrival hadn't gone unnoticed with more than a dozen rough-looking alpha males. Their malefactor was staring in my direction; the intensity of their gaze was palpable. Never had I felt so intimidated. Every one of us was stripped of our shoelaces and belts so that no one could hang themselves or someone else for that matter!

I leaned forward and struggled to look through the small wire re-enforced glass window on the cell door. I squinted and could barely make out the numbers on the clock hanging on the wall directly outside our cell. 5:49 AM "Ugh," I groaned. I had only been a few minutes, and yet it felt like hours had elapsed. I was certain that the placement of the clock was no accident. It was likely a slow form of real torture. The tick, tick, ticking was sure to agitate the testosterone levels of this motley crew of cellmates.

My imagination was drowning me as negative thoughts poured into my head. There is a saying that the anticipation of death is worse than death itself. Being drowned in the cell commode was probably more fun than the cacophony of self-talk and images that were at play in my head.

"Holy shit! I'm in Jail!" I whispered under my breath as reality set in. I cannot lose my spot at The First Tee or any clients because of this situation. "Could life get any worse?" I repeatedly asked myself, struggling to put my situation into perspective.

Immediately, thoughts of my friend and renowned sports better Mr. William "Billy" Walters floated through my mind. *Billy* and I had met in 1998 at Bighorn Golf Club while caddying in a "High Dollar Cash Game." *Billy* was mostly known for his gambling prowess and was arguably the G.O.A.T for sports betting.

I had become very close with *Billy* and couldn't help but shed tears when the news came out that Billy had been sentenced to five years at a minimum-security prison in Pensacola, Florida for insider trading.

The very same insider trading case involved PGA Tour- Super Star Philly Mick, aka *Lefty.* Sadly, *Lefty* had invoked his Fifth Amendment rights and possibly withheld information that might have cleared *Billy* of wrongdoing. This was the second documented time in so many months that *Lefty* would send another human to prison in an effort to save his own ass. It was deplorable. The Judge disregarded *Lefty* as a main character in the trial, even though his name was mentioned 122 times.

I took a couple of deep breaths knowing that things could get worse. I closed my eyes and attempted to relax my mind as it drifted back to earlier in the day...

After giving two golf lessons in the morning and getting in a little work on my own game, I headed up to play 18 holes of golf at Bighorn Golf Club in a "cash game" with an old sponsor and his friend Ash.

Bighorn Golf Club is a spectacular 36 Hole Championship golf facility and is listed in the Top 50 Private Clubs In America. This 1,150-acre facility was founded by Westinghouse in 1991, then repurchased in 1996 by a small group of investors including R.D. "Dee" Hubbard and former PGA Tour veteran Jim Colbert.

Bighorn became my office in December 1997 after I quit my real job to chase my childhood dream. I always thought that if I had to work, this certainly couldn't be worse than being choked by a tie and having to look at cubicles all day long. And the view from the club held a sublime beauty.

I had been nursing a pesky shoulder injury and Dr. Tom Iwashita was my secret weapon. He was relatively unknown in golf circles. I first heard about all the great things he did when I was rapping with a Pro Volleyball player at the valet at Bighorn. Dr. Tom was the Team Doctor for the Olympic Volleyball team in Brazil. He is much more than just a chiropractor and integrates several modalities which makes his practice completely unique and powerfully effective. His Myofascial Release, while particularly painful when applied, was the one thing that freed my muscles and ligaments and helped to relieve my pain and expand my range of motion. After getting my shoulder and body back to prime form, I felt healthy and knew nothing could stop me from having a super low round today.

Making putts were going to be paramount since this was my first round of golf in a while. I had been attempting to rest my just newly healed body before my upcoming departure to the **Champion Tour Regional Qualifying School**, aka *"Tour School."*

To say that I was very comfortable on the greens at Bighorn Golf Club was an understatement since I had seen both courses damn near 500 times each. Reading putts for $25,000 or more, was the norm while working with Las Vegas gamblers like William "Billy" Walters and Paris "Butch" Holmes.

Billy, a car dealer and bookmaker from Mumfordville, Kentucky was my W-2 employer for five years and a great friend.

Butch was a commodities broker from Texas, a golf addict, and my main golf sponsor in '01. And, he was a lot like Jack in that sense that he was a G.O.A.T and documented as the most successful golf gambler in history. Beating the likes of Dewey Tomko, Doyle Brunson, and Bobby Baldwin out of millions on the links; *Butch* would play anyone for One Million $ Nassau in his prime.

Bighorn Golf Club was where I witnessed my first real golf hustle, and it offered me an inside look at a recession-proof facility. I had pulled a few strings to get my friends on this super private playground for the ultra-rich and famous; It was the least I could do since one of the guys was my former sponsor in '05.

My morning lessons schedule at The First Tee had taken a little longer than expected. Arriving a few minutes later than planned, I pulled into the valet just as my playing partners Jeff Snow aka "Snowman" and Nick Ash came strolling out of the main entrance.

"You boys look like a couple of old hustlers looking for a pigeon?" I blurted out laughingly.

"Andrew Arleau, you look great. How the hell are you?" Snowman shouted as we began walking towards each other.

"I am as happy as a camel on Wednesdays," I chuckled. "How you boy's been?" I continued, "*Snowman*, how's the family?"

Snowman snickered back, "Everyone is great, thanks for asking." We embraced each other with a manly squeeze, "Who's our fourth player?" I asked.

Snowman, with a wry smile on his face, said, "*Double A*," You're not going believe who we ran into last night at dinner... Sam!"

"Sam?" I questioned. "Yes, your old caddie from the Tour?" My stomach sank as I realized what *Snowman* was saying. Sam was a name I wanted to keep in the past. The wounds were still festering under my skin like a carcinoma that I hoped would never reappear.

"Hey Pal, thanks for the invite." A voice came from behind me- I turned around to my displeasure... *Sam Sarazen* in the flesh. I hoped my lips didn't move as I internally muttered, *Fuck Me!*

Half grinning at Sam I jumped into the driver side of the golf cart thinking I couldn't possibly bear riding with him. Trying to be cool I said, "Jeff, why don't you throw your sticks on with me... Sam, you can roll with Ash." The tacit motivation of this move was probably clear to everyone. This was my golf course and I was in control.

I continued, "Let's get warmed up, we are on the tee soon." I didn't actually know if we were next up or not, but sometimes in golf just like in poker; you need to bluff.

With a hint of sarcasm, Sam proclaimed, “Sounds great pro,” as he strapped his clubs on with Ash.

Sam was a very good tour caddie, and he touted an extensive PGA Tour resume’ having worked for many great players on tour including H.O.F. great Jack Sherpa. Sam caddied for me almost three seasons and to be honest, there were times when I was almost convinced Sam was the reason I was playing well at the time.

There was no doubting that Sam was a great caddie, but unfortunately, Sam had a BIG head, an inflated ego, and an even bigger mouth. Worse than his bravado and arrogance were the rumors that constantly swirled around the tour that Sam was talking smack behind my back. He claimed I was cheap and on top of that, said I didn’t have the temperament to make the Tour. This wasn’t particularly shocking since most tour caddies were cutthroat. Loyalty was not their “long game,” and there they didn’t hesitate to inform me of his slanderous game.

The truth was, I was paying for Sam to stay with me in a two-room suite when we traveled together. It was standard fare along with $200 per day cash on the days that he caddied. Thinking this was pretty good pay, especially considering I didn’t have a fully exempt PGA Tour card, I quickly grew tired of his presence and particularly his cockiness. After a couple of poor finishes, and similar to what many tour players do with caddies, I had to let him go.

After a brief warm-up, we arrived at the first tee with Ash and Sam blurted out confidently, "Our cart against yours for $100 Nassau four ways, two down auto presses?" Smiling and cockily I looked over at *Snowman* who was nodding in approval, "80% of your handicap and you got a bet!" I said.

Ash added, "That's fine; how about $50 KP's (closest to the pin) and sand-saves, plus $100 birdies?" *Snowman* nodded as we were of the same mind and responded with "Yes and yes!" I loved the feeling of being connected with my partner. Our connection or "collective vibe" if you will, felt like it was building an etheric shield and deflecting the jarring energy being projected by Sam.

As we prepared to tee off, it was time for Sam to attempt to swing back the pendulum of control to his side. These swings, pun intended, were common in golf. Momentum swings of confidence were huge, having it on your side could make the difference between winning a $1K and losing $1K; which was a $2K reversal in fortune.

He wasted no time talking smack. Unfortunately for me, he knew all of the psychological weaknesses in my psyche and in my game. "Hey Andrew, what are you working on regarding the ole' swing?" He paused for a second and then continued, "*Double A's* always working on something NEW you know" My hands shook for a second, as I replayed that last statement in my head a few times. Probably the only thing worse than your opponent's smack was when your inner talk was smacking you back.

Sam knew I disliked conversations regarding swing technique before playing. I knew he was trying to get into my head, and while inwardly it was bothering me, outwardly I smiled and began looking down the fairway for a good target. I read in some motivational book; I think one written by Tony Robbins, that words were only seven percent of communication and the rest was body language, tone, and all the other non-verbal stuff. As much as possible I tried to let my body do the talking for me.

"How about those *rabbit ears*, you still have those?" Sam whispered to Ash in his best Elmer Fudd voice... "*Double A* really hates whispering when he is shooting, so be *bery bery* quiet." Ash smiled and began to hoot... "Now that's funny!"

Not so amused, I stared down the fairway. Scanning into the distance, I located a small tree beyond the green. I locked ON like a laser sight from a gun and put a red dot on the target. Staring solely at my target without a single blink, I began scanning my body. Feeling my toes and feet, and then working my way up through my body connecting to the earth made me feel strong and grounded. Pressing my two fingers together to start my personal computer so to speak, it brought me into a positively anchored, flowing state. I was calm and cool like a sniper.

Lock. Walk. Waggle. Relax... these words echoed over and over again slowly repeating themselves in my head, as I began walking into my shot. My mental routine started up automatically just as I had practiced all that week to replace thoughts of technique.

I shifted my attention from my target to the ball without a single technical thought as I addressed the shot. I took one final look at my target to validate my alignment. Back to the ball "commit," I whispered as I slowly drew the club back... "Smack." Dead in the center of my TaylorMade M6 Tour driver, the spring effect of the twist face technology was unbelievable as I watched my tee shot fly like a jet down the right side of the fairway.

Swinging the pendulum back to our side, with moxie I asked, "Anybody want the long drive for $100?" I laughed as I taunted Sam and Ash. I watched both of their bodies slightly retreat. The boxing motto of *kill the body and the head will fall,* came to mind as my lips smiled by themselves. They all knew that I was a much better longer driver of the ball off the tee. Neither responded verbally; I smiled directly at Sam as I knew this was an uppercut mentality. Round One or rather Hole One, I bemused was ours.

I was very proud of myself for being mentally tough and not getting distracted by Sam's nonsense. Sam had done his best throughout the day to distract me from playing well, from walking behind me during a shot, whispering when I putted, and even pulling the

Velcro on his glove twice while I chipped. Both times he laughingly attempting to apologize, as if his actions hadn't been purposeful. With each amateurish attempt, the pendulum swung farther to our side.

The match ended very one-sidedly as *Snowman* and I crushed our opponents six ways to Sunday on the front nine, winning 5 - 3 & 1. I rattled off FOUR, yes FOUR birdies that nine and EIGHT birdies total for the day. It wouldn't be my greatest ball-striking round, however. My $750 custom Kenny Giannini tour putter didn't disappoint. With only 26 putts on the day, my partner Snowman and I would win eight bets overall, plus $200 each in "side junk" for a grand total of $1,000 each. Even though Sam was often a distraction, I was proud of myself for rising above it.

After the round, we found ourselves standing in the valet area waiting for the cars to be pulled around. We agreed to discuss meeting up at the Red Barn aka, *"The 5 Star Dive Bar"* for a cocktail and to square up the debt. It was very apparent that Sam was maddened, and he was silent for a change. I metaphorically stuck the knife in and twisted.

"Sam. Come on now, the bet is ALWAYS won on the first tee; you should know that!"

The pendulum was fully erect on our side. I chirped out "Follow me guys," while jumping into my car as I led the group back out the main gate. *Snowman* and Ash were in the SUV behind me, Sam in his Porsche bringing up the rear. Just like the cars behind me, this incredible day of golf, family and friends were in the rear-view mirror.

~ 29 ~

The Crisis

Still stuck in this semi-drunk half-hungover bad dream, the screech of the cell door being reopened commanded my attention and goosebumps arose on my already cold arms.

"Patrick Swift, you've been bailed out!" The Sergeant barked.

Barely awake, the guy next to me inadvertently kicked my foot, as he pushed himself off the floor using the wall. The odor of whiskey was so thick you could almost imagine it seeping out of his pores into the air... I was now back to full consciousness.

"I'm out of here bitches," the guy mumbled and stumbled as he headed towards the cell exit. Bailed out. That was something I was hoping would be in my near future too, now that sobriety had begun to set-in.

While the jail cell slowly emptied, my headspace was flooded by an ocean of depression. I was so in the dumps that I even contemplated not going to *Tour School. What a piece of shit,* I thought to myself as I sank back into my corner and closed my eyes thinking, where *did I make my wrong turn? How did I let this happen? Could I lose my job?*

My mind was out of control, thoughts drifting with no end in sight, as I floated even further back to the very start of my day.

This day had begun like any other day, around 5 AM. "I love you," Arya whispered into my ear, "brought you some coffee." Then she gave me a soft, wet kiss. I was damn lucky to regularly start my days off this way. Damn lucky! Much like the first drive in a round of golf, I always thought that how your morning started would create positive momentum for the day. My "daily" was a far-off distant land compared to my current cell conditions. Arya was far better looking than Arturo, the tatted-up gang member, who was sporting a wife beater, black shorts, bruises, and a black eye.

Arya Lyte, in addition to being my wife, was a loving mother to three beautiful children and was also the Spa and Fitness Director at Tamarisk Country Club. Arya originally crafted her trade in the fitness and wellness industry as the Spa Director aka (the Commodore) at the world-famous Parker Palm Springs before being hired by Tamarisk C.C.

Arya is absolutely the most positive human being I know and my angel, always wanting to know the intricate details of my day. She often left me encouraging notes on the bathroom counter like "Remember your own greatness and never let anyone steal your joy."

I sipped coffee as we planned her Parents' 48th year anniversary at Ruth's Chris Steakhouse and discussed the possibility of going out on the town afterward. "I really like the Red Barn, don't you?" Arya said. "Sounds great to me My Love," I affectionately replied. The Red Barn was known for great live entertainment and cheap drinks. I was more than content with our plan.

We spent a good thirty minutes listening to each other. As usual, the time flew by. "Wow, it's 6:30 AM and I've got kids to get ready, lunches to pack, laundry to switch and fold," she said. I watched Arya hurriedly disappear down the hallway as the morning fire drill hand began. She was our family's Fire Chief. Arya began herding all the kids out of bed, racing them first into the shower, then down for breakfast, and then out the door in order to get them to school by 6:55 AM. I quickly jumped into the shower, closed my eyes, and tried to see my day and how I wanted it to play out. I visualized my day just like I did in golf.

I'd been chasing the dream of playing on the PGA Tour for almost 13 years and despite having some shoulder issues and not playing competitively for the last few years, I still had this feeling inside that one day I'd be competitive again.

Since meeting Dr. Tom Iwashita at Bighorn my shoulder was even stronger than it was before turning 50 years old back in August. He had also miraculously addressed my old neck and upper back pain. *Tour School* was just a few days away and loomed large in the forefront of my mind. I was really looking forward to playing golf today and getting outside with friends and maybe even doing a little gambling. I thought to myself, *Today was a great day to work on my mental routine, let the mind run free of technique.*

As a tribute to “Seve” I dressed in head to toe black attire, including my favorite Francis Edward belt. Exiting the closet, I grabbed my all black *“Live Lucky”* Black Clover hat. There was no way I was going to forget my lucky hat today!

Leaving the house for Palm Desert, a little earlier than usual to avoid traffic, I would arrive at the First Tee Training facility about 30 minutes before my students arrived. I was giddy and couldn’t wait to hit a few balls and find my rhythm and tempo before heading up the mountain to play at the Bighorn Golf Club at 12:30 PM.

My first student Pema arrived a few minutes late, for which I gruffly scolded her, “You do realize I have other students after you?” Sometimes I could be an ass. “I am so sorry, but there was an accident right outside the entrance,” Pema explained apologetically. “Please… don’t be late again!” I softly barked as I took a deep breath.

Around 7 to 8 swings into Pema’s warm-up, I couldn’t help but notice how much she had improved since our last session. My mood moved from agitation to elation, much like the pendulum swing in a golf game. “Wow, somebody has been putting in the work.” I praised. Thoroughly impressed at her improvements, continuing to pump her up mentally I said, “You could get a full ride golf scholarship like the Evans Scholarship if you keep up your hard work. “Trust me on this!” She shyly smiled in acknowledgment, her inner pendulum, also swayed back to confidence, as she continued about her practice session.

Midway through my training session with Pema, I began a long and detailed discussion about rhythm and tempo. I stressed to her how everyone has their own speed in which they walk, talk, swing, etc. I said, "If you're a fast walker and quicker talker your tempo and pace will usually be fairly fast and vice versa. Basically, your rhythm should be yours, just like my rhythm is mine," I stated.

Pema nodded with a slightly unsure look about her. "Is there an example of the method that you personally use to manage your tempo?" With a childlike grin, I chirped out, "Why, yes there is, and I have just the story for you."

"I found my rhythm 15 years ago in my second year as a professional. It was in the 1st round of a 72-hole event called, The Sun Bum-Choco Mountain Open." Pema stopped hitting shots, and I could see I had her undivided attention, as I continued. "I had opened with a -7 under par 65 in blustery conditions and extremely difficult pin locations. Feeling pretty good about my round, and as we headed into the scorer area, you couldn't help but see the name at the top of the leaderboard--my favorite player ever, Jack Sherpa. Jack had shot an unbelievable **64,** -8 under par. Only six players broke par that day and only three golfers shot in the 60s. It was an amazing round of golf!"

Jack Sherpa, widely known as "The Ram" was a veteran lifetime member of the PGA Tour. He was widely known for his short game prowess. Not only was Jack *my Idol, but* he was also the *Course Record Holder* at over a dozen golf courses in the area. His most notable score included a 57 at his home course Him-Ah- Lay- Ah Country Club which was another 12.7 miles further up the mountain beyond Bighorn Golf Club.

I headed into the snack shop, sending my then new caddie Sam Sarazen to find us a spot on the range while I grabbed us a quick lunch. I selected Sam as my caddie since he had an extensive resume' and worked for some of the best players on the PGA Tour including Jack Sherpa, himself.

I didn't know all the dirty details--I just knew that Sam was abruptly fired by Jack after seven years for what was rumored to be theft of some kind. One thing was for certain though; Sam knew that he drove Jack nuts, and therefore I should have been more cautious before sending Sam to the practice area where the two of them would meet up. There is no question that I should have foreseen what was about to happen next.

As I reached the range area, I could see Sam waving his arms back and forth like he was lost at sea and had just sighted his first airplane in two weeks. "Hey Pro, there's a great spot!" Sam pointed, yelling across the range. The grin on his face told me all I needed to know.

Sam slammed my overloaded, 50 plus pound TaylorMade Tour staff-bag to the ground with a loud crash, setting up camp in the hitting stall directly behind Jack. Sam didn't see eye to eye with his old boss and had been trying to get into Jack's head since retribution was his mentality.

Approaching the stall with my index finger on my lips, motioning for Sam to shush, I turned towards Jack and quietly uttered, "Hello Mr. Sherpa, pretty tough conditions out there?"

As he half turned towards me, I had captured his attention, and I continued with another question, "How was your game today?" Jack completely turned now and began walking towards me. With a long pull off his Marlboro Red and a broad smile, smoke billowing out his nose and mouth he began, "Andrew, correct?" I nodded *yes,* utterly shocked he even knew my name.

"Andrew, anybody can play under ideal conditions," he stated with a rarified swagger and confidence. He took another long pull off his nicotine stick, as he cogently continued, "I miss-clubbed twice, and my waggle was a little off."

While I processed his jaw-dropping words of wisdom, I was completely dumbfounded by his response considering Jack had shot -8 under par 64 in tough windy conditions. *I mean seriously... miss-clubs and waggles.*

"Pema," I continued watching attentively as my idol, *my freakin' idol* began working the alignment sticks on the ground like a fanatic, standing directly behind the ball, and tweaking the stick to perfect alignment prior to each ball. He went through his entire routine before hitting each ball." Just like a freakin' machine! I had absorbed a lifetime of golf in those moments like he was a walking Demigod."

Pema replied, "I had read that Mr. Ben Hogan was fanatical about his waggle. I guess I never used or thought of the waggle in that manner." "Do you follow Pema?" I softly, but emphatically asked making sure I still had her attention. Pema nodded, as I continued rambling with excitement over my once in a lifetime experience, I could see I had her 100% attention. Her eyes were filled with intent as her inner keyboard was typing every word into her mental register.

Continuing with my lesson I said, "Mr. Sherpa didn't work on his Technique or Mechanics during tournaments, he worked on *BASIC* Fundamentals: Alignment, grip, ball position, posture, balance, and his *waggle*. This helped me tremendously to reduce shoulder, arm, and hand tension pre-shot as well as create great rhythm and tempo, which is what started this whole conversation."

Reaching into my pocket for my phone to check the time, I realized we had gone a few minutes over. Bensen, my next lesson, had already arrived and was wisely warming up.

I quickly wrapped the session up, "Pema, I would like you to work on your course management, as well as to have minimal technical thoughts while playing on the golf course." I continued "Thoughts of technique create tension and reduce your athleticism and speed;

furthermore, Inner and outer tension create tightness and tightness kills... Work on your *waggle*!"

As Pema packed up her gear, I reminded her, "Our next lesson will be about how to avoid unnecessary risks. "Thank you, Andrew," Pema yelled with a smile as she headed towards the clubhouse. *Oh, how ironic that would be considering my current situation!* I deliberated.

I finished my morning lesson by helping Bensen with his short-game. We had been working hard on the full swing for two full seasons, and it was now time to start letting his game flow without thoughts of technique.

It was just before 12 o'clock. I had cleaned up my area and packed up my training devices. With an extra $300 cash added to my betting budget, I made the quick 10-minute drive up the mountain to Bighorn Golf Club, ready to do some gambling. I mused how I was lucky that most people's quitting time was 5 o'clock, and mine was noon! *Golf isn't just my business, it's my hobby* I grinned internally as I quoted Lee Trevino in my head.

Armed with *my rhythm, my waggle* and a very HOT custom crafted Kenny Giannini putter, my partner *Snowman* and I made fast work of the other team and beat them out of $1,000 each. Completely elated with my play I couldn't help being braggadocious and talking shit to Sam as we walked off the 18th green.

The group and I decided to meet after golf at The Red Barn, my favorite *5 Star Dive Bar.* With happy hour generously convening from 8 AM to 8 PM, this was *the place* golfing minions would frequent to square-up on golf debts, listen to tunes, and consume cheap drinks.

Snowman, Ash and I arrived around the same time. As we approached the bar, Ash shouted over the jukebox, “Three lite beers please.”

As we sat there sipping our suds and waiting for Sam to arrive, I could sense that Ash was a little upset. He was upset about the beating, but he was especially pissed by all the shit-talking I’d been giving him and Sam all day.

“I cannot believe how poorly I played,” Ash whined as he handed *Snowman* $1,000 cash across the table. “All square here.” Ash proclaimed with a wry smile.

I couldn’t help myself as I talked more shit, “That shot you hit on six was so bad that had you been eating you would have missed your mouth with the fork.”

Snowman and I laughed hysterically as I continued my verbal routing. I now had free rent in Ash’s head.

“I recommend taking two weeks off and then quitting golf all together?” Bwhahahahahaha! *Snowman* and I busted out in laughter.

Ash wasn't about to take my BS. "Buy me a shot and shut your cake hole" Ash barked out.

"Thanks for inviting Sam Sarazen, *Snowman!*" Ash's face wrinkled in disgust as he continued his whine, "Sam was worse than even not having a partner." I had to agree with Ash as the match felt like it was three against one.

Flagging down the bartender, I yelled over the music, "Hey Kevin, three Jager bombs please."

Ash's paying *Snowman* $1,000 burned into my retinas. I thought I could even feel and hear them sizzle. I was anxiously waiting to get paid myself. I couldn't but help thinking, where the hell is Sam?

I leaned towards *Snowman*, "Speaking of Sam... where the hell is, he?" I said as I looked at the clock on my phone, "I haven't missed any calls, and it's been almost 10 minutes." "Is it possible he would no show?" *Snowman* said. "Maybe," I shrugged my shoulders knowing deep down he wasn't coming.

"Final-Final boys I have to go, dinner with the family." "Cheers!" "Kampai!" We slammed our shot glasses together, "down the hatch."

Out of respect to Sam Sarazen, I hadn't mentioned to anyone that we had parted ways a few years back at the end of my last full-time season. The rumors about Sam stealing and scamming were serious. It was beginning to affect my trust, and I didn't want to be his next victim, so I had to let him go.

Stepping out the back door as I headed to my car, I decided to call Sam. The phone rang and rang and after 15 rings finally went to voicemail. *Leave a message after the BEEP.*

"You asshole, I cannot believe you didn't show up to pay up!" Sliding into my car, I spewed anger as I hung up and violently spiked my phone on the passenger seat almost hitting the ceiling on the bounce.

Wasn't this the reason I didn't want him around? I thought to myself as my heart beat heavily.

I had driven about halfway home and was finally calming down when my phone began to flash and buzz. I had put it on silent mode during the round so as not to interrupt anyone. Hoping it was Sam, I looked at the caller ID. It was my Boss from Bighorn. *What could he possibly want?* I thought.

"Hello, this is Andrew," I answered. "Andrew, this is Mr. Darman from the club." He continued, "Your friend Sam Sarazen came as your guest today, correct?" "Yes?" I questioned intently and concernedly. "Well, he didn't pay his green fees!" I quickly interjected, "Mr. Darman, are you kidding me? This is a joke, right?" I asked. "No, and that's not all. Our men's locker room manager said he saw Sam stuffing his pockets full of amenities from the men's locker room." "Oh my god..." I bellowed. I listened quietly as Mr. Darman respectfully told me this wouldn't happen again. Feeling completely embarrassed after hanging up the phone, I hoped that this didn't mean zero guests in my future.

In our separate cars, Arya and I both arrived home around 5:30 PM where I proceeded to vent about my day; Sam Sarazen taking off without paying, and the call from Mr. Darman. "Can you believe that jerk would come up to my place of work and pull that kind of stunt." I blurted. "I mean seriously I am so pissed off right now. He owes me $1,000!" Arya listened carefully until I had spilled the entire deal. She was such a sweetheart, allowing me to diffuse these toxins from my emotional system. She wrapped her arms around me and said, "Let it go My Love." As she looked at me with her amazing green eyes, I melted. "You are right Lover, let's go have some fun tonight."

After my rant came to an end, and with some of the pressure released I looked over at the clock, "Wow, I better get ready babe, we don't have a lot of time." I paused… "Would you like to share a drink while we get ready?" "Sounds great my love," Arya said with her beautiful smile.

Although I'd had a beer and a shot, I was starting to feel some pain in my shoulder and was wanting another drink in hopes it would reduce my shoulder pain. I didn't want a DUI, so I wisely chose to wait to have another at Ruth's Chris with dinner.

I pulled out my phone and ordered three kids pizzas, breadsticks and a two liter of root beer on my Domino's app. We quickly shot out the door in a race to make it to Ruth's Chris for a 6:30 reservation to celebrate Arya's parents' 48th anniversary.

~ 42 ~

My 22-year-old son Dayton, from my second marriage, had just graduated from UC Irvine and was in town to take a break from the beach madness. We decided to invite him along to Ruth's Chris now that he was of legal age to have libations. We had a great dinner at Ruth's, a couple of bottles of wine and a ton of great food.

After dinner, we decided we would cruise over to arguably the hottest after-golf hangouts fittingly named "The Birdie Nest." Upon arriving, we noticed the line to get inside was winding around the side of the building. "Wow, this is insane," Arya said.

I tapped Arya on the shoulder, "Let's go to the Red Barn as we discussed earlier. I think Grady James is playing tonight." I whispered. "Sounds amazing," Arya whispered back with her sexy voice. We had a plan as we promptly got back in the car and went to The Red Barn.

We pulled into the back parking lot. Already pushing the limits of my blood alcohol levels in the drive over to the Red Barn, I mentioned to Arya and Dayton, "I think we should leave the car here and UBER home," we all concurred.

"Bartender whatever they want on my tab!" Everyone ordered drinks and then proceeded to mingle through the heavy crowd.

Dayton had invited his mom Tara and her guy-friend to join us at The Red Barn. Tara was my second ex-wife and not exactly my date of choice but I tried to make nice and enjoy the conversation and music. Attempting to ease the tension, I immediately ordered another Jager Bomb.

As the evening progressed, I did my best to have fun and go with the flow. However, I couldn't stop thinking about Sam Sarazen, the money he owed me, and what he had done at Bighorn. I was incensed at the very thought that he had come to my club, embarrassed me, threatened my job, and to add insult to injury; he no-showed on his $1,000 pay-off at The Red Barn earlier in the day.

"Bartender, I'll have another shot!" I yelled over the band as my blood boiled with anger.

About an hour had passed, and I began roaming around the bar running into Arya and Tara, "Have you ladies seen Dayton?" "No, we haven't seen him." Tara said, "Is everything ok?" I looked her calmly in the eyes and said, "I'll find him." I walked outside to the patio almost running into Dayton on the outside to the smoking area out back. "You ok Bud?" I asked Dayton. "I'm absolutely amazing," he chimed. Attempting to walk towards me the smell of tobacco drifted into my nostrils as he stumbled into the wall. It was obvious Dayton was feeling no pain. "Be careful son," I said in a stern but loving voice. "I'm just having fun Pops," Dayton said with a smile, as he headed back inside.

Finding myself a bar stool, I ordered myself another Jager Bomb and water. For a moment, I mentally calculated *I think this is my third.*

This was really the first time all day that I had finally slowed down and relaxed. I closed my eyes and felt the vibe of Grady James' music. Tapping my foot on the stool, rocking to the beats, I then scanned the bar just noticing Arya as she headed outside. I could see a look of distress, as she placed the phone against her ear. I was too far away, and the music was way too loud to hear her conversation. I was eager to find out what was going on, but I had a gut feeling something was wrong.

Her oldest daughter Nara Lyte's calls had gone unnoticed on three separate occasions. Two were when we were at Ruth's Chris and one while we were at the Red Barn. Nara is a brain tumor survivor and takes seizure meds daily as a preventative measure. Although it had been a while since her last seizure, Arya was always on high alert.

Arya turned to me as she hung up the line, "We have to go. We have to go now!" she blurted. Arya's word came out jumbled with the adrenaline rush. With playing the music in the background, all I could clearly hear were the keywords *Nara, head, and nausea.* These were the same symptoms from her last episode. Seeing Arya's distressed look, at that moment, I added fuel to the fire by thinking of Sam Sarazen, the $1,000, and Mr. Darman. I fueled the incendiary explosion in my mind as I replayed these scenes over and over again in my head. Combining the noxious cocktail of the adrenaline rush and lingering suppressed aggravation from the day, I made the blameworthy decision to drive us home.

The time was 12:26 AM. I had driven about five of the 20 miles back home. Not happy that we had to leave so suddenly, Dayton was starting to get loud and very argumentative in the back seat. He was teetering on full-scale belligerent. "Hey!" I yelled into the back seat. I remember glaring into the rearview mirror inquiring about his loud tone. As Dayton and Arya began to verbally altercate, I became more and more distracted. I said, "What is your problem?" "Don't you dare raise your voice at Arya." I still wasn't sure what was going on between them.

Having always had night driving issues, I might as well have been wearing a blindfold. "Look-out!" Arya screamed. Crunch, Bang, Boom, impact!!!! A black low-profile car was stopped at the red light in front of us. I had been distracted looking into the rearview mirror and engaging in verbal warfare. I couldn't believe it, I had rear-ended another car, *WTF!!!*

Pull over and be responsible, my left brain was telling me; however, the other side had different plans. I threw the vehicle into reverse, backed up, slammed it back into drive and lit up the tires leaving a cloud of smoke 100 feet in the air as I barreled towards home. "What are you doing? Pull over!" Arya and Dayton pleaded. Adrenaline pumping into jackhammer mode. I roared out "Shut the FUCK UP, I'm taking you home." Without a doubt, I knew then that I was going to jail and was determined to get Arya to her baby Nara first. I continued to chirp, "Remember your daughter... remember?" "I said I would get you home and that's the end of it." I made a commitment to get Arya home and was going to follow through, figuring out that the consequences would be the same regardless.

It turns out that the person who owned the vehicle that I slammed into was a retired government employee and had 911 on speed dial. He followed me from a distance and had the fuzz on the phone the whole time. As I pulled through the gate to our home, I told Arya and Dayton, “Get ready and I will let you out!” Within seconds seven police cars converged on us, slamming on their brakes, sirens blaring, lights flashing. It was like watching a 4th of July fireworks climax. The smell of burnt rubber was in the air.

All I could think was, *please don’t embarrass your family.* I continued past the house just around the corner, one-half block away. I placed my hand on Dayton’s leg as I leaned over and gave Arya a kiss. “Goodnight, I love you both.” I tried to softly breathe out the words “Everything will be ok…”

I pulled on the handle and pushed the door open with my foot as officers converged. “Get your hands in the air, now, do it NOW!” Before even presenting my driver’s license, I was jerked out of my car and slammed to the ground.

“You have the right to remain silent, anything you say, Blah, Blah, Blah…” or that’s the way it sounded.

After frisking me they cuffed me and stuffed me into the back of the squad car with the cuffs digging into my wrists. I could feel the blood running down my arms where I had raspberry burns from being used as a mop across the asphalt. Forced into the back of a cop car, I was quickly reminded these vehicles weren't made for comfort.

Handcuffed and left in the back of the car for 2.5 hours I was finally taken to urgent care to give blood and then placed back in the car where I sat cuffed for yet another 1.5 hours, which was deserved, I guess.

It had been over 24 hours since my EPIC day began, and here I was in-processed, fingerprinted, and booked. Laying on the ice-cold floor, I was completely wiped out, running purely on adrenaline, my brain flooding with negative thoughts.

Did Arya know where I was being held? What if I had killed someone? Feeling disgusted and pity for myself, I asked. *How can I get out of this suffering?*

~ 48 ~

The Dream

Sitting on the frigid floor trying to keep my mind busy, I began to reflect upon my prior career as an (ATC) Air Traffic Controller. I remembered some arduous scenarios during my tenure that created some sleepless nights. Additionally, for seven years I had worked a challenging schedule with a mixture of day, swing and mid-shifts. Over time this schedule jacked with my Circadian rhythms spun my sleep schedule around and caused sleep issues. I was, unfortunately, one of the 48% in the world who suffered from insomnia.

Often, I resorted to drinking alcohol in the evening to relax and help me sleep. ATC employees weren't allowed to take any prescription medication for Rx for pain or sleep.

After leaving my job as an Air Traffic Controller to chase my dream as a professional golfer, I resorted to smoking pot to help me to sleep, since alcohol wasn't the best for the putting stroke over long-term.

I tried those plop-plop fizz-fizz wafers a few times, and they had worked ok, especially when having sinus or allergy problems. Finally, feeling exhausted, my body was craving sleep.

I went to a sleep specialist a few years prior, and, she immediately asked me if I had done any sleep training or had worked with a hypnotherapist? "I haven't, but I am interested," I replied since I was into anything that would help my sleepless nights.

The sleep specialist was of little help. I later referred to as the “sheep specialist”, because about all she did was tell me to count sheep.

Eventually, after working with a Hypnotherapist, I was able to use several visual and auditory techniques to help me fall asleep.

I would have never imagined myself sleeping on a hard-ass cold floor. Regardless, I had made my bed and now would sleep in it! I attempted to implement one of the techniques I was taught. I started by rolling my closed eyes upwards towards the sky and began counting backward from 10 to 1. I began to count, ten, nine, eight, seven, six, f... I was out.

Out... out cold as I hit the ground beneath me. I was now sleeping. I found myself in a dream that seemed so real. In fact, it was more real than real. The thought, *so real is similar to surreal,* popped into my head.

Next to me was a glass of those plop-fizzy white-wafer things on the nightstand. From a distance, a golden orb of light appeared and began moving closer into my awareness. Its emergence from total darkness shook me into an even more intense state. The bright light orb, now visible, to my closed inner eyes, morphed into a Golden Buddha. “Andrew,” the Buddha said as he leaned in next to me, “The life you pleaded for when you fell asleep is possible, it does exist!”

I was clearly hearing the words of a Buddha speaking to me. It was more real than a conversation with a human. *What in the world?"* I pondered.

The Buddha continued, "while you think that this physical world you live in is real, it is merely an illusion. It is an illusion within your mind."

I had never encountered an experience like this before, and I began wondering *Is this really happening?* This was the first time I had had a dream this real. I immediately asked, "Why are you here?" Before the Buddha had a chance to engage, I continued to blab, "Why are you helping me?"

The Buddha, while he didn't move his lips, seemed to be grinning and said with grace and timbre, unlike anything I had ever heard before, "Because you asked." He said he was moved by my deep desire to escape from misery, and that his caring nature allowed him to intervene when cries for help warranted it. "Andrew, you have the ability to get out of suffering."

I took a moment to absorb what he had just said. *Could he read my mind?* I began wondering. *"Will I ever get off this merry go round of highs and lows, or will the rest of my life be consigned to yet more rounds of anguish and suffering?"* I said to the Buddha, "If Sam Sarazen where to pay me the $1,000 he owes me--now that might get me out of suffering." I chuckled as I looked over at the Buddha. He clearly wasn't amused, and his facial expression remained unchanged. I often used humor as a way of breaking the ice, but there wasn't any ice in this interaction. It was more like ether than ice.

"The problem is that you over-identify with the transitory world around you, Andrew. You believe your world is real. *It is an illusion.* The Buddhists call this illusion *Maya.* You are so caught up in the mode of ego, pride, survival, emotions, and beliefs, that your inner peace is rarely experienced." He sagaciously paused to allow me to take in the above. It was like drinking from a heavenly firehouse.

I took a moment as I processed before commenting. "Kind of like stressing out when you're going to be late to a meeting, and then upon arriving you realize the person you are to be meeting with isn't even there yet?" I said in an inquisitive tone. I tried to answer my own intimation by saying, "Creating an illusion in my head that never existed, and then worrying about it... *Maya*, I think I get it."

"Yes," the Buddha said and while he didn't move his head, I could swear he had nodded.

While in this dream I began to sense something inside me was changing. My body seemed to unload with a lightening of sorts occurring. This was an amazing experience. *"Wow, what elation!"* I thought.

For much of my life, I had always felt reactive and defensive, living the highs of the ups and the depression or low of the downs. There had been many instances in my life that were filled with high hopes of a glorious outcome, whether it was a new sponsorship opportunity or winning a golf tournament.

There had also been chaos during my previous home-life that had created self-doubt as to whether my golf game was good enough to compete at the highest level. It seemed I was always looking over my shoulder waiting for the next mishap or near miss to occur. I always seemed to have a back-up plan in case of failure. The last *eleventh hour* of *disappointment* sent my emotions into a tailspin followed by a crash landing. Nevertheless, I almost always reacted harshly, negatively, and self-destructively after a poor showing or set-back.

To make matters worse I would phone home between events to the Ex-wife and the conversation would almost always go something like, “How much money did you win?” or “Hope your vacation is going ok,” and that bugged the hell out of me. Regardless, it was me getting in my own way, creating illusions that didn’t even exist and I had no right placing the blame elsewhere. I was a mess deep down and was ready for a way out. Luckily for the both of us, Tara and I divorced in ‘08.

The internal *lightness* was gaining momentum, as I started feeling substantial improvement. This pendulum move toward inner peace was far greater than any pendulum swing in the material world. It was like comparing Mount Everest to a hill in Kansas. Rather than feeling heavy and congested, which led to my standard defensive and guarded responses, I felt open and proactive. The feeling of being proactive gave me a new-found hope that I might be able to create the reality the Buddha was suggesting. In some indiscernible way, I intuitively knew what was happening.

His gracious presence initiated a domino effect, clearing the view to enable me to see my life from a different perspective. My physical illusion was changing. I felt I had a better handle on my reality. *Of course, this whole thing was a dream, and maybe I was just deluding myself,* I laughed inwardly. *If I was chuckling during this time of crisis, maybe this whole dream was real after all? Or, maybe my "jail reality" was the actual dream?"* The worlds of *Maya (*illusion), dreaming and dreaming of a dream were morphing in an out, leaving me in a state of awe and wanting to learn more.

The Buddha sat patiently looking at me, so I decided to ask another question, "How can I change it? This *Maya* thing, the illusion I mean?"

The Buddha, again appearing to grin without grinning said, "Andrew, it is about changing your perceptions. I will teach you **Three Priceless Techniques.** The more you practice these **Techniques** in your daily life the easier they will become, and the less stressful your life will be. Your life will have much more peace, meaning, ease, and you'll help those around you, as well." I chortled to myself, as it sounded a lot like a famous golf quote from Lee Trevino, "The more I practice, the luckier I get."

I was uncertain yet captivated. *I really have the power to transform those who surround me? And, with only **Three Techniques**?* I contemplated and wanted to hear more, yet a part of me was feeling hesitant to change. I was still not convinced.

"Honestly the word Technique is a word I use with *caution* regarding teaching and playing golf." Looking over at the Buddha I continued, "One must be very careful not to get too technical and to understand how golf techniques or mechanics are applied in order to *feel* during a round of golf."

The Buddha listened with no facial expression as my rant continued.

"I always make sure my students know when and where the practicing or visualizing of a technique is appropriate." I continued, "Each of my students is given a specific set of drills to be executed on the practice range only."

"This technique is then honed through repetition of drills in order to help correlate that drill to a *feel*."

"Providing the player with a *feel* to take to the course is paramount to success. Focusing on golf mechanics on the course kills athleticism and speed."

After finishing my rant, I ignorantly wondered if this conversation was driving the Buddha crazy. Yet I continued to mull around the idea in my head of **The Three Priceless Techniques**. For a moment I realized I was, in essence, trying to tell the Buddha how to do his job. *Wow, that is a lot of hubris,* I mused. I'm qualified to teach people how to golf, but NOT how to teach a Buddha how to be a better Teacher. Oh man, this Buddha was right, I was living in an illusion (or delusion.) I was living in the illusion even while I was dreaming with this Buddha.

I quickly realized that I had better shut up, be receptive, start listening and be a good student. After all, as good as it could be learning from my idol Jack Sherpa, I now had a Buddha teaching me! *What would the Buddha be asking of me?* I wondered. *Would he address my drinking and pot smoking? I guess I could drink a little less, maybe smoke a little less.*

Now feeling defensive I said, "I have great willpower, Buddha." Then I paused. "I stopped using chewing tobacco 4.5 years ago after a 30 plus year habit." I paused looking for any kind of reaction, "That proves I have willpower because I can quit anytime I want... Right?" I said this while smiling and searching for the slightest reaction from the Buddha.

The Buddha silently waited for me to finish... He then carried on "Not only will these **Techniques** help your golf and your life; these **Techniques** will also help inspire and motivate others to duplicate them. As more people participate, you and others will have the power to reshape the world in a giant *Buddha Field,* or, in your case, a *Buddha Fairway,* lined with lotus flowers."

"Buddha Field... What the heck is a *Buddha Field?"* While I might have sounded disrespectful, my voice was now infused with inquisitiveness. My mind

attempted to visualize a *Buddha Field,* or even a *Buddha Fairway* for that matter.

"Good question," the pleased Buddha replied. "I'll explain that in a moment. However, for you to figure out where you are going, we first need to review where you've been!"

The Beginning

In a whoosh, the Buddha and I were sitting on an imaginary balcony. Looking down on a scene from my past, I could see the calendar on the wall, and it read 1977. That year was hard to forget since Elvis Presley, and Bing Crosby had both passed away earlier that summer.

More importantly, this was also the year that my father's golfing idol, Mr. Al Geiberger earned his improved nickname *"Mr. 59."* That round was so incredible that even Mr. Lee Trevino was quoted saying *"Al Geiberger should have to take a test and prove he is a member of the human race."*

Earlier in Al's career, he was often referred to as "The Peanut Butter Kid" or "Skippy" due to his penchant for munching on PB sandwiches throughout his round. *Mr. 59,* however, was a much more suitable moniker since Al was the first golfer ever to shoot sub 60 for 18 holes.

Mr. 59, coincidently, turned professional in 1959. He claimed 30 professional wins in his career, 11 coming on the **PGA Tour**, and another 10 on the **Champions Tour.** *Mr. 59* famously won the **PGA Championship** in 1966, the **Players Championship** in 1975, as well as two-second place, finishes in the 1969 and 1976 **U.S. Open Championships.**

"I am shocked *Mr. 59* hadn't been inducted into the H.O.F.," I proclaimed, speaking directly to the Buddha as if he might lend an influential hand in the induction process. "I mean seriously, shooting "59" on a par 72, in 1977?" "Wow... Think about that for a second. He accomplished all of this without all of the modern-day golf and training technologies."

The Buddha nodded with the approval of my *Mr. 59* history lesson as he redirected my sleep deprived, slightly OCD attention back to the clock on the wall. The time read 4:30 AM as we intently watched my eight-year-old self. I struggled to make out the toy in my hands. I thought to myself, *what is it that I am playing with?* I leaned towards the Buddha to get a better view as the scene now shifted to my Grandparent's house.

Our family tradition for many of my younger years was to spend Christmas Eve with family at my grandparent's house on my father's side. All the brothers and sisters would show up for the event and exchange gifts, and each kid would get to pick one from under the tree. I knew one thing for sure; my Uncle Daryl always gave us the best gifts.

As all the children stood in line to find a gift, I remember scanning under the tree looking for a box from my favorite uncle, Uncle Daryl. I blurted, "Boom, over to the right... there you go!" from what I was now mentally referring to as the *Buddha Balcony.* I was amusing myself, as I attempted to direct my younger self. The Buddha remained stoically blissful as he shifted the scene back to the basement back once we returned home on Christmas day.

The Buddha looked over towards me and gestured, "Do you remember now?" He continued, "This is a significant moment in your life." "Really?" I responded as we continued watching. "That's right! I wanted to be a pilot and fly high above the ground like the birds." The Buddha seemed to acknowledge my revelation, and we continued watching. "I remember now. That was an airport game with a plane that flew in circles, lowering close to the ground for doing touch and go's and low approaches." I smiled as I recalled my obsession with model airplanes. "I had always wanted to be a pilot. Sadly, I was disqualified for medical reasons. Everything happens for a reason I guess," I said to the Buddha. I laughed at myself, for I was *telling* the Buddha "Everything happens for a reason." If I was this arrogant with an enlightened being---a Buddha--I must have been exceedingly arrogant with mortal men. It was like going into hyperspace in a Star Wars movie as my dream shifted again, fading away from the basement.

Whoosh... We were in the front yard of our Franklin Street house, and I saw my father and me with a golf club and wiffle balls all over the backyard. "Oh," I exuberantly said to the Buddha with a smile, "I remember this part, he was teaching me how to grip a golf club. I snickered, "Just like **The Three Priceless Techniques** you've offered to teach me; my father taught me *Three Simple Gripping Methods*." He reminded me, "The grip is one of the most important components of the game, if not the most *important!"*

My father physically placed my hands on the handle of the golf club showing me as he explained the *Three Simple Gripping Methods:* "Grip Number One is *The Overlap Grip*, aka, The Henry "Vardon Grip," Grip Number Two is the *Interlock Grip* used by Jack and Tiger." Gently he moved my hands, "And finally Grip Number Three is the *10 Finger Grip,* and it is just like it sounds."

My father continued this grip education by saying, "Son, your front or lead hand should hold the grip like a hammer squeezing only with the pinky and ring fingers." He then emphasized "There is no perfect grip choice. Whichever grip you feel gives you the most leverage and strength as both hands work together, that is the correct grip for you."

I remember choosing the interlock grip without hesitation, mostly because my idol Jack Sherpa used that grip. I was very excited to watch this moment in time and to see the care and love my father used in showing me the grip as well as other facets of the game. That was the moment I was *hooked on the game of golf forever,* and I would start dreaming of making this my life's work someday.

With a whoosh, the entire scene changed...

I could see a small group of kids out in front of the Plaza mini-mart. There were giant piles of snow pushed against the building due to the freezing temps.

Like typical boys from the northern part of the country, none of us were wearing jackets. I spotted myself standing on the end, the shortest of the group by far. Everyone huddled around the big guy like we were prepping for 2nd down in the red zone. I remember we were going on a beer run. My buddy "Jaybird" was collecting all the cash from the huddle because he knew a guy who would buy us beer before the basketball game. There was a dance that evening after the game, and we all thought it would be fun to get a little buzz before the dance. We had collected $21, which I remember bought us eight 40 Oz bottles of OLDE English 800 at $1.36 each.

"Combat Ken," whose name was completely based on his wardrobe choice of always wearing camouflage, was the guy all the local kids went to for beer. He lived across the street in a creepy six-story apartment building called the Conrad Arms. I remember this building having only one elevator which went up to the center of the building. Lee, *Jaybird,* and I went into the cage-like elevator and up to the 4th floor to see Ken. Greenbacks in hand and ready to party, Ken was more than happy to get us beer for his $10 tip. Ken came around the building by the dumpster. The and grins on our faces were priceless. "Beers for all!" Ken proclaimed as he handed us four large brown bags.

I looked over at the Buddha and started talking, hoping to find comfort with my excuse. "What do you expect? We didn't have much to do in the winter," I explained. Neither changing his facial expression nor moving; he seemed to give me a reassuring nod. The Buddha fast-forwarded three hours to after the game.

While the fast forward was occurring, I realized that *Combat Ken* with the beers wasn't smiling at us like I thought I had experienced when I was a kid. I now saw the scene through adult eyes. I could see the sadness in his eyes, the wrinkles on his face, the craggy lips, the unwashed clothes, and the dirt under his fingernails. I began realizing why he only wore camouflage, as those were probably the only clothes that he had. He was most assuredly a veteran, and I could now see and feel his suffering. Whew... This new-found wisdom was a bit too much to bear. I was also not used to operating from this level of compassion.

Standing on the *Buddha Balcony,* we looked down on our high school field next to the gym. Five young mischievous boys with 40-ounce beers in hand were clanking their beers in a toast. "Cheers gentleman, to fun times ahead!" Cheers bellowed from the group as the underage drinkers banged the bottles to the evening ahead. We made fast work on the beers and headed into the dance. As I recall, I was buzzing and couldn't wait to hit the dance floor.

We arrived inside, and the dance floor was bumping. I began dancing with my friend Kim as Frankie Goes to Hollywood flowed out of the speakers. "You smell like beer," Kim stated as she stepped back. "Whatever girl... Mind your own business," I said as I turned and headed to the men's room. Luckily for me, the restroom was empty as I stared into the mirror. My eyes bloodshot and glossy, you could see the sweat running into my eyes as I used a towel to wipe my face. Making my way back out to the dance floor, I ran into *Jaybird.*

"Have you seen Lee?" I slurred over the blaring of the music. "Nope, haven't seen him," *Jaybird* looked around the room, as I sat down just for a moment. Whoa, the room began to spin*, that Old English 800 was kicking my ass.* All I wanted to do was take a nap. *Just five minutes I told myself,* as I dozed off.

I was not sure how much time had passed as I woke with Lee pulling me up from the chair. "Grab ahold of him," Lee barked out to the others surrounding me. "We need to get him out of here now!" *Jaybird* said. We headed towards the side exit and everything looked to be going my way when I was stopped at the exit by security. "You have an I.D.?" the security guard asked. I emptied my pockets and wallet into his hands hoping he would let me go. "Ok boys leave him with me and go back to your girlfriends," the guard commanded--I had been BUSTED.

Security had two volunteer parents walk me to the couch just outside Principle Gordon's office, as they waited for my parents to arrive and come bail me out.

From the *Buddha Balcony,* we watched as my younger self lay there outside of Principal Gordon's office, with Phil Collins 1981 hit song *In the Air Tonight* faintly echoing down the hallway. Seeing myself get busted was super embarrassing and difficult to re-watch. I wondered what the Buddha must be thinking as he watched along.

"Your Parents will be here soon," Gordon stated. I had just started to fall asleep as he spoke into my ear, and the room began spinning... "Braaaaap," I proceed to blow chunks on Principal Gordon's shoes and all over the tile floor.

I was completely disgusted watching the me from 30 years ago. The Buddha, like usual, was clearly unimpressed and showing no other expression except a gentle smile with a pervasively peaceful countenance.

My parents arrived shortly after, and with one eye open, I could see them talking with Gordon in the hall and looking over at me. "We will have to suspend him," said Gordon. I sniggered from the *Buddha Balcony,* as I watched my immature self, reach into my back pocket to throw a can of Copenhagen behind the couch, then pass out again.

My mom continued to speak with Principal Gordon as my dad came over to the couch, picked me up, and slung me over his shoulder. He carried me to his El Camino where I sat in the open-air bed. Yes, 15 degrees in the back of the El Camino..., I had earned an open-air ride home. I wish I could say it was a cold ride, but I couldn't tell you, because I was passed out!

I was a member of the Varsity Wrestling Team as just a freshman. The Letter that I earned was taken away. I later was suspended and spent 10 school days at a desk just outside the Principal's office.

This time when I looked over at the Buddha, I was embarrassed. I was embarrassed at how irresponsible I had been when it came to alcohol. It now dawned on me that while I had an excuse for my behavior when I was underage, there were no excuses for its improper use as an adult. For the first time in the *Buddha Dream,* this most surreal of places, I was experiencing shame and guilt. The Buddha maintained his smile as if to say, "Very good." The Buddha was showing me these scenes as if we are watching a drama and I was the main character. A drama it most certainly was.

The Joy-Ride

We returned again to the spring of '85 when I had just finished shooting 68 in my first High School tournament. As a freshman playing Varsity, I was looking pretty good. A 68 was pretty darn good! The Tri-City Invitational was always our first event and touted the best teams in the state. The Invitational was the annual start to the season.

We had taken two teams composed of five players each, ranging from freshman to seniors, and with the addition of two adults, there were twelve of us in total. While the older players and coach were checking the leaderboard, I had decided that I was going to take the rest of the team to the 7-11 for jumbo Slurpees. I was always in charge of the situation even as a wee freshman.

From the *Buddha Balcony,* I watched my younger self climb into the driver's side of the 12-passenger high school van. I began to chuckle, thinking *this is funny,* as I watched my younger self start the van--without hesitation. My golfing minions climbed aboard for what was sure to be an eventful ride. Everyone was in the van--with me, the Driver's-License-less Freshman commandeering this escapade. No one seemed to care as we proceeded down the hill towards our sweet candy and beverage bliss.

Coming out of the store I remember simultaneously both the adrenaline rush and the knot in my stomach knowing that if things went wrong--I would be a criminal. I had *borrowed* the van without a license, all to impress my teammates. I displayed the same moxie as a kid as I had when I beat Sam Sarazen at Bighorn.

I quickly herded my young minions into the van, and we rapidly headed back to the course before the coach and the older teammates returned. Boys being boys there was certainly a fair share of farts along the way. Marc Morello, a senior and quite the rabble-rouser, coined the term "goxing." He learned in a science class that GOX was gaseous oxygen. Hence, *goxing* was born and it was part of our team vernacular. We arrived back safely without a hiccup, or at least so I thought.

The Buddha and I continued our view from the *Buddha Balcony,* as my younger self and my freshman flock returned to the parking lot and then sat patiently slurping our ill-gotten frozen delights.

As we continued watching, I could see my best friend Lee returning to the van after a trip to the men's locker room for a bladder check. Obviously amped up on sugar from his Coke-flavored Slurpee, Lee decided to have a little fun of his own, as if taking the van for a joy ride wasn't enough.

After several verbal encounters between Lee and the opposing team from the Valley who were in the bus next to ours, Lee snatched the fire extinguisher from its holder and leaped back out of the van. With a THWACK, BANG, and a BOOM, Lee kicked open the opposing team's van doors and fired the powdery retardant into their van. "Eat my dust!" Lee bellowed. I couldn't help snickering from the *Buddha Balcony* as the young golfers poured out of their van like a swarm of hornets with its nest on fire.

We must have been ignorant to think Coach wouldn't notice the gigantic Slurpee cups throughout the van and the thick dust from the overspray. The very last extinguisher blast had blown directly into our open van window. It was like a white sandstorm had hit our bus.

Our Coach was no dummy and immediately started questioning us, "Who drove the van?" We all looked at each other, and everyone with rehearsed stories acted as if they no knowledge of the events at hand. Not a word was uttered. We would face our demise over the weekend as Lee told "his version" of the story in order to receive a lesser charge. You could hear a pin drop on the 90-minute ride home. The following week I lost, yet another Varsity Letter. My parents were again very disappointed with me, and I was as well.

The Buddha sat there speechless. I was at a loss for words. Having forgotten that part of my colorful Varsity letterman past, I looked over at the Buddha for comfort and guidance. Not changing his facial expression in any way, his expression exuded peace and warmth that gave me some modicum of reassurance that I might be able to have a better future and a better life.

The College Days

Swiftly, we jumped to another scene. I saw my half-bearded face sitting at a small enclosed desk that was connected to a wall. Immediately, I knew the Buddha had taken me back to my college days. From the *Buddha Balcony,* looking upon my younger collegiate self, many memories and emotions flooded in. Much like when I empathically felt *Combat Ken's* emotions, I was even more sensitive now. My sensory acuity was at a new level. I recalled the term *sentient beings,* and now had a greater understanding of what sentient actually meant.

Before the days of Blue Rays and DVD's, I began to remember sending VHS videos of my golf swing to all of the recruiting coaches in hopes of getting my college education paid for. My parents were in the process of buying the family business, and it was obvious to me and everyone, that I would need to get a scholarship if I wanted to go to college. Having to play golf to finance my education at such at an early age certainly helped me cope with the financial stresses later on in my adulthood. My father and brother had enlisted in the USAF and proudly served our country, and I was hoping to be the first family member to attend a four-year university.

Finally, at the last moment, the phone rang, with Weber State offering me a full-ride golf education.

The Buddha and I watched the scene of me answering the phone. From the *Buddha Balcony,* I got a little misty-eyed watching the simultaneous relief and joy emanating from my young face. *I had done it! There had been a lot to overcome to achieve this milestone, and I earned it.*

My college career was cut short due to a lack of focus on my classes and the tragic death of my teammate, mentor, and great friend Mark Dougherty. Mark had been a senior. It was his second year after spending two years at Scottsdale Community College where he was a 1st Team All American during his sophomore year. Mark had been chosen by the coach to keep me on-track and show me the ropes, basically to babysit me and keep him informed of my progress.

Mark and I had attended plenty of parties that school year, however, this particular night we were attending a fraternity party at a downtown hotel. Neither of us had plans to pledge. Mark and I had grown to be very close friends and shared many of the same interests.

We had picked up a dime bag of some bomb-ass weed en route to a party. After arriving downtown at the hotel parking area, we fired up a joint and sat in the shadows on Mark's bumper. We smoked the entire thing before heading inside. The party lasted a couple of hours, and we had more than enough to drink and smoke.

Wanting to be responsible Mark said, "I would rather not drive. Let's try and find a ride home," I agreed. We started to ask around for a ride to our apartment near campus when a couple of guys came out of the party. Mark approached them to ask for a ride back to the pad. To this day I am still unsure what was said as the bigger guy recoiled back to punch Mark. Getting caught up in the tense nature of the scene, I yelled, "Look-out Mark!" from the *Buddha Balcony.* The Buddha softly placed his hand on my shoulder. "Remember this is an illusion," the Buddha explained. "You are still holding on to your friend. You are still holding on to a lot of suffering around this experience. We will talk more about what Buddhists call *Samsara* later." Still shaking a little, I pensively asked, "Is this treatable?" The Buddha, again without changing his facial expression, gently and said, "Yes, I can show you how."

Just like unpausing a movie, the scene continued as Mark lost his balance and fell backward. His head struck the ground with a smack. *I will never forget the deadly sound of Mark's head slamming into the cement like a bowling ball that had been dropped from chest high.* Watching the bounce from the *Buddha Balcony* this time around made the experience even more surreal. Blood began to puddle under his head as I ran towards the two guys who were by now jumping into their car parked 25 feet away. Before they sped off, I reached into the vehicle to grab the passenger and was quickly thrown out as the car raced away. There were no cell phones at the time, so I ran to the pay phone near the elevator and quickly called 911.

Mark had lost a lot of blood and was rushed to the hospital. He suffered from brain trauma and was placed on life support until he was pronounced brain dead 24 hours later. His toxicology report showed THC in his system. The authorities barraged me with questions.

It was the first time I had experienced a real death other than that of family members passing from old age. I had never been a fan of funerals, and I hated seeing my best friend being buried. I remember saying to myself: *Life is way too short and all I want to do is have fun.* This attitude didn't work well over the next few months, as I left school prior to the end of the year and never returned.

I looked over at the Buddha looking for some kind of sympathy or reaction. I was a little frustrated and distraught now. *I mean come on... M*y scholarship had been cut short over this incident, and it was the sole reason I had ended up in the military and become an Aeronautical Science ATC specialist. The Buddha seemed to be smiling even more and was his always contented and peaceful self. The Buddha explained, "All of these experiences of wins, losses, and challenges in life are what shape the way a person behaves and reacts. We must learn as much from failure as we do from success. In the eyes of eternity, this scene is merely the blink of an eye. The equivalent of a body shedding a dirty set of clothes."

In self-pity I thought, m*y life is over, and I am a failure.* I retreated home to live with my parents with my tail between my legs. The Buddha and I watched the scene of reconvening with my family.

Upon my arrival, my dad Vern offered me a job working in the family business--Arleau Transfer and Storage. It was the hardest work on earth, in my opinion, and I quickly looked for alternatives to make money in my spare time. I liked to gamble, thus I sought out opportunities on the golf course as well as playing darts at a local bar. The job was heavy in terms of the physical labor, but the weight on my shoulders in carrying out the penance was far more laborious.

I knew my education was important, so I registered at the local Junior College in an effort to finish my Associate's degree. I only had a few credit hours left and was certain it wouldn't be a problem to finish. That was before I realized how many of my friends hadn't left town and were attending the JC as well.

Between the house parties, the pool, and ping-pong betting in the student lounge, I didn't have time for class as I was skipping regularly. My grades quickly took a turn for the worse as I preferred participating in social gatherings and gambling opportunities for side cash. I also often frequented women's volleyball and basketball games where my best buddies *Jaybird,* Lee, and I would shotgun cheap beers in the parking lot before going into the games to pick up girls or to "hunt fluff" as we called it back then.

As I watched the scenes with the Buddha, I started reflecting on the meaning of life. *Life is fragile and could be gone at any moment. Why are we here? Is this all there is? First birth, then partying and all its consequences, then work that wasn't fun, and then death, which seemed like a painful way to escape it all. What happens after this life?*

A few months had elapsed into the 2nd quarter on what seemed like any other Friday. *Jaybird,* Lee, and I met as usual in the northwest-most corner of the college parking area at 7:30 AM. In the parking lot, Danny Mills and Dave Bayonet were talking to *Jaybird* and Lee. Danny's dad was a fish and game warden. He and Danny, my Dad and I had often hunted together in the past.

The biggest attention grabber was the two snowmobiles in the bed of *Jaybird's* truck. It was snowing quite heavily, and I could see this wasn't going to be just any other Friday of skipping school, as the discussion of heading to Mission Peak was the topic. "Hey *Double A*, what up bud-zo?" said Danny. Lee quickly interrupted, "*Jaybird* and I are taking his dad's sleds up to the ridge. Want to go?" Lee continued, "Danny and Dave are going as well." As he gestured towards them with a pause and a squint in his eye and teased, "Or are you on your period this week?" The other three snickered.

It had been a while since I had snowmobiled. "I will sit this one out and go on the next run pal," I said laughing as I graciously declined to take the first run. *Jaybird* and Lee shook their heads as they laughed turning towards the snowmobiles. I remember now wishing I would have gone snowmobiling. The moments following shifted the direction of my life.

"Well, I am definitely not going to sit here in the cold. Jump into my truck boys. I've got a few beers," Danny offered. I couldn't wait to get some heat on my feet. I had worn tennis shoes and was ill prepared to be in the snow, let alone go snowmobiling.

Danny had purchased his ridiculously large metallic blue truck back around our sophomore year in high school and had slowly added a roll bar, lift kit, and 44" tires and rims. This monster could go just about anywhere imaginable and in it was where the trouble began.

The Buddha and I watched, Dave and I climb, and I mean climb, into Danny's super-sized truck. I sat in the middle as Dave pulled the passenger door shut. As Danny started up the beast he asked, "Either of you ever heard of *Suicide Road?*" I shook my head sideways to indicate NO as did Dave. I remember thinking, *do I really want to know? "Are you kidding me?"* With a shocked look, Danny screamed into my ear, "*Suicide Road* here we come. This is going to be awesome," Danny said as he tossed each of us a beer and we headed further up the mountain.

While sitting in the *Buddha Balcony*, I looked over at the Buddha, maybe to center myself. I didn't' know I was still learning. During the prior major scene, I had watched the tragic death of my best friend and now I knew what was coming.

We drove about ten minutes further up the hill as the terrain became steeper and the trees denser. "How far are we going?" I asked Danny. "Just a bit further, have another beer and relax," Danny barked, "It's just up ahead, besides those guys will be sledding for at least an hour." I didn't want to be judged, so I just sat back and drank my beer.

Upon arrival at the end of the road, Danny shut off his truck off and jumped out, keys in hand. Dave and I were staring at a gigantic chain spanning from one tree to another blocking the entrance of this old logging road called *Suicide Road.* Loggers had used this road for expressing logs down to the river and sometimes as a shortcut back to camp.

"Wait right here, I need to unlock this entry," he chirped from outside his truck.

I recall looking straight out the front window of Danny's truck and seeing nothing at first. I Leaned forward to get a better view of the so-called road headed straight up the mountain. I would have been even more nervous had I not downed five beers since leaving the JC campus. "Let's do this!" Dave yelled out. I threw on a fake smile and pumped my fist, even though deep down, I was scared as I had ever been in my 20 years on earth.

Danny jumped back in his monster of a truck and began pumping the throttle as we crept towards the steep football field length incline. Danny leaned over towards me and whispered, "You ready my brother?" I wasn't ready by any means as I nodded and said, "Let's go." Danny jammed the gas pedal to the floor as his truck began barreling up the hill.

As we ascended *Suicide Road,* I glanced to the right only to see an even steeper drop-off into certain death. Danny had the pedal to the so-called metal as we ripped towards the top of the mountain. Suddenly I could feel the tires begin to slip in the semi-frozen, yet muddy conditions. "Uh Oh, that's not good," Danny blurted out, as we came to a complete halt a few feet from the top.

As I watched this scene of my past self, I couldn't help but laugh because I knew the outcome. "This was a scary moment for me," I said to the Buddha. "A real crossroads in my life," I remember thinking when it happened that for sure at that moment, *my life was over*.

We had stopped for a bit before we began slowly sliding backward with nowhere to go but straight back. One false move and we could have rolled potentially to our deaths.

I must have been breathing hard as Danny jabbed my ribcage and proclaimed, "Relax *Double A,* this isn't my first rodeo." I was freaking out. Danny, on the other hand, was as cool as the ice on the ground of the hill. He slowly backed his ginormous truck down the hill.

Dave hadn't said a peep since about halfway up and had a grip on the *Oh Shit* handle in Danny's truck so hard you could see the white on his knuckles.

I let out a giant sigh of relief as we reached the bottom. "Wow, *Double A*, you were really worried, weren't you?" Danny jabbed. I didn't respond as I sat silently in shock.

"That was awesome," Dave responded as he finally released the handle. I looked over at Dave in amazement, "You're kidding right?" "Don't act like that was fun," I rebutted to Dave as we started to bump each other. "Shut the hell up!" Danny belted out, "You're both a couple of pussies!"

Dave and I sat silently in the truck as Danny jumped out of the truck to lock up *Suicide Road.* I didn't speak a word as we drove back to our rendezvous point. I did ponder that night where I was going with my life, and one thing was a certain, I would never go on *Suicide Road* again.

The Buddha and I continued watching until my younger self returned home that evening. I remember being very quiet as I continued my thoughts about my future. *I think I will follow in my father and brother's footsteps and join the United States Air force.* I would head to the Recruiter's Office the next Monday morning.

The Professional Golfer

The Buddha and I returned to the *Buddha Balcony,* a place that I was becoming ever more familiar, with each scene transition, as I experienced new aspects of my being. We flashed forward to the year I turned professional in '96. While '96 will be more known for Prince Charles and Lady Diana getting a divorce, my turning pro mostly went unnoticed

My father Vern had flown out to Raleigh Durham International in North Carolina to help drive my Mitsubishi Eclipse back to Washington State where I was raised. He arrived with a carry-on and his golf clubs only to be disappointed by a fluke snowstorm and freezing temperatures.

Even though I had been stationed at Pope AFB in Fayetteville, NC for the last 1.5 years, I had mostly been TDY (Temporary Duty) for the past 10 months and didn't really know the area very well. Our thoughts of golfing were now tempered as we drank coffee and planned our 55-hour drive home through 10 states at a Starbucks Coffee just outside Raleigh.

I turned in the direction of the Buddha, my thoughts began narrating the scene.

I had just returned from *Operation Deliberate Force*, Aviano, Italy and had applied for and received an early release from active duty to chase my childhood dream. This was not an easy decision since I had a nice paying job as an Air Traffic Controller. However, I just couldn't stand being around most of the people I was working with or for. It seemed like everyone I worked with thought they "were the best" and liked to toot their own horns all the time.

I commonly referred to this as "God Complex." I had to laugh at my realization when I contemplated just how many times, further I gave advice to the Buddha. Maybe interacting with some of these people had rubbed off on me. I started contemplating how the people we associate with influence us both positively and negatively. I appreciated that in the *Buddha Balcony* I was much wiser and could see things without the lens of misconceptions through which I had previously viewed my world. The Buddha lens was a combination of the Hubble Telescope and a microscope that could zoom into a resolution of less than an angstrom.

I really started laughing now at my "Mini-God complex" and noted that I should ask him sometime about the difference between Buddha and a God. As I looked over to the Buddha, he was reading my thoughts and could certainly feel my emotions. While I couldn't read him, I believed he was laughing inside too. "Being stuck in the darkness and cold of the Radar Room in my old Air Force job, I couldn't wait to get out and get started working on my golf game. With an Honorable Discharge from the USAF, I returned to my hometown to regroup and hopefully find a sponsor to help finance my dream career.

In my first few years as a professional, I had a learning curve playing in Canada and Asia. I knew my skill set was better than most but needed to be put to a more prominent test. Quickly learning it was a must to find a way to go low at least once per week, shooting even par wasn't going to get it done. This learning curve wouldn't come easily either. A friend of mine who eventually became very successful in the insurance business would always encourage me by saying, "The first year you learn, the second year you burn and the third you earn!"

To again quote Lee Trevino, "The more I practice, the luckier I get." That mentality wouldn't work here either unless I was 100% committed and disciplined to the process. That's what playing at the highest level required.

As I stood with the Buddha high above my past, I observed intently as the scenes from golfing around the world changed quickly in front of us. We continued watching the different scenarios of my past self, playing golf tournament after golf tournament. It was this moment that I started to remember my only goal…Winning!

As we continued down this slide show into my past, the images began to slow. The scene was '05 and I immediately remembered the moment as I saw myself lying on an Asian dragon designed couch with my eyes wide open. Sports Performance Hypnotist, Gina Mae "Magic" Coffman was standing over me, her familiar medallion swinging in front of me. That year was arguably one of my better seasons as a professional, as I had qualified for several Tour events and made more money than ever after working with Gina and her *Magic!*

As Gina swung the medallion in front of my face, she began to speak. "We will start by closing your eyes, counting backward from 10 to 1 as you internally find your way to the 1st tee of your favorite golf club."

"10, 9, 8, 7... Gina tapped me on the forehead as she continued, "You are an amazing golfer with a huge heart, 5, 4, "Now, imagine yourself teeing off, 3, 2, 1." Gina paused for a second, "You are playing the entire course with flow with ease. With each swing, you become even more relaxed and fluid."

In my mind, I began playing each shot one after the other. The feeling of striking the ball felt very real as I made my way around the course enamored by the utter beauty I imagined as I made the turn to the back nine. The smell of the Stillwater Cove was almost real as I played the holes along the water. I further understood that whether I was under hypnosis, dreaming, in real life, or on the *Buddha Balcony* they were are all very similar in that the experience was taking place in my mind. I was able to access different parts of my consciousness in different ways in each. The concept that the Buddha shared with me that this was all in my mind was making even more sense now.

I had just made my way up the hill as I stood on the 13th tee and I could barely hear Gina whispering next to me, "Remember Andrew, golf is not a perfect game and you must learn to detach from outcomes." Gina continued speaking softly in my ear, "If a putt doesn't go into the hole that doesn't mean you didn't make YOUR putt."

Gina continued whispering NLP (Neuro-Linguistic Programming) in my ear, as I approached the 18th green at Pebble Beach, I could almost feel the spray hit my face as I imagined the ocean that crashed against the cement wall near the greenside bunker. Gina's voice was faint as she whispered, "As you finish your round you will become even more aware of your surroundings and slowly open your eyes." She tapped me on the forehead again. As I came back from my round at Pebble, I felt accomplished even though it was just imagery in my head.

"How do you feel?" Gina asked. "Amazing!" I said. "I just shot 57!" "Excellent, did you make any mistakes?" She inquired. I laughed, "Yes I made a bogey on 14, just like the last time I played there." Gina smiled as she asked, "Have you ever made a putt that didn't go in the hole?" I thought for a second, "I'm not sure what you mean?" Gina grinned, as she explained, she kind of reminded me of a *Junior Buddha,* "You know, you hit the putt exactly over your spot with perfect pace… ¾ of the ball goes down into the cup before being spit out onto the lip." I paused, "Yeah I guess so…" Gina laughed, "I guess what I'm saying is you might hit a perfect putt that doesn't go in." She continued, "That doesn't mean you didn't make your putt." I smiled realizing she had whispered that earlier during my round, "I understand now, thank you for that lesson."

Gina bowed, again very *Junior Buddha*-like, as she gestured to the front door, "Today's session is over my friend, see you in two weeks." I looked over at the Buddha as he appeared to be fully engaged in the dream. "I will have an audio tape for your next session," Gina said. "Thank you." I nodded appreciatively.

The Buddha waved his hand in front of me as we jumped ahead two days...

Armed with a fresh positive perspective, I caught a flight from LAX to Chicago on Monday to qualify for the final Western Open. The Western Open was the oldest PGA tour event on tour and would be a Fed-ex cup event the next year.

With only three spots available in a 98-man field I knew it would require a low score to make it to Thursday's first round. Upon arrival at the course, I went directly into the golf shop and asked the gal behind the counter, "Do you have your course record posted anywhere?" The shop attendant pointed in the direction of the hallway as she stated, "Just down the hall on the left wall near the exit."

I wandered into the hallway and found the official scorecard hanging on the wall with Tour player Jerry Smith's signature on the bottom. Jerry had shot a course record 68 the previous year in the U.S. Regional to qualify for the U.S. Open.

"68, wow, this course must be tough," I whispered under my breath as I studied the card. I noticed he had taken advantage of all four par 5's and had also played a flawless bogey-free round. I remember thinking of this great image in my head I couldn't wait for Monday morning.

I woke up early Monday morning to stretch my body and grab a light breakfast at the course. I met Sam Sarazen on the putting green about 30 minutes before we teed off. "You like the course Pro?" Sam asked me. "I do," I responded with a calm demeanor.

I placed an alignment stick on the ground as I began stroking putts parallel to the stick line to a tee stuck into the ground. This would help me by visually reaffirming I was seeing the line and hitting my spot with the putter prior to play.

I had hit about 10 or so putts when Sam said, "Stroke looks good Pro!" "Thanks, bud, it feels good" I responded.

Closing my eyes, without thought, I began putting the ball across the green to get a feel for the speed and distance of my *stock putting stroke.* I continued rolling the ball one direction, then back the other direction, pacing the distance after each putt. My *stock putting stroke* at this course was 25' feet since the greens were pretty buttery. I also refer to this 25' distance as the *freed-up zone*.

Just as I was finishing my session, Sam alerted me, "Ten minutes Pro." He added. I nodded as I picked up my practice balls and we headed towards the first tee.

I was nervous as I stood on the 1st tee behind my teed-up ball. I confidently located my target and went through my routine. My drive started into a dogleg left more than I had planned slightly pull hooking it next to the practice range. “Oops…” “Is that O.B. over there?” I asked. Sam quickly responded, “You’re good; see the green flag?” I hadn’t noticed the volunteer standing on the corner holding up the green flag. I smiled and without a word handed Sam, my driver, as we started our 4 ½ hour walk.

As we approached the ball, yardage book in hand, we weighed all the options. I realized we didn’t have much of a shot without taking unnecessary risk. I remembered a friend who made his living as a day trader used to say, “The key to making money is to not lose it,” meaning take care of your downside, let your profits run. That was applicable in this situation for sure.

“Pins back left correct?” I asked Sam, with my hand resting on the 4 iron as I contemplated hitting a giant slice around the trees from about 175 yards. “Yes sir,” Sam responded. Without hesitation, I looked over at Sam and pulled out my sand wedge.

“Looks like a sand wedge.” “Do you like 75 yards at that big pine across the fairway?” “Perfect,” Sam replied, nodding his head in agreement.

I pitched the ball back into play, exactly 100 yards from the cup. I subsequently followed that shot with the same sand wedge to six feet and sank the putt for par. This was just the kind of start I had envisioned with birdies on both par fives on this difficult front nine, making the turn in -2, 34.

The 10th hole is a narrow par 4 at 335 yards, I decided to hit a driver and smashed it straight towards the back-right flag. My playing partners lay up to around 75 yards from the green since the hole was very narrow and sloped off severely into the trees on the right. The temperature was starting to warm-up, so Sam and I walked the left tree line in the shade as we watched the others play into the green.

Knowing I could get to the front part of the green with my driver, we walked slowly all the way up to the green hoping to see my ball on the putting surface and a chance for eagle two on this short par four. "I thought it was straight at the pin." Sam said, "Agreed."

As we began to approach the five-minute mark, the old maximum time to search for a lost ball, a rules official drove up asking, "You guys ok?" I responded back with a smile, "Sure could use a ride back to the tee," I said with a smile. "Hop in Andrew, you're lucky I arrived." I turned to Sam as he tossed me a new ball.

"You know the rules official is the only one that can give you a ride in competition, right?" I didn't respond immediately as I was focused on keeping an even keel with my emotions today. "Is that right?" I said as I jumped out of the cart back at the tee.

The group behind us on the tee was waiting patiently, as I went through my routine prepping to hit my third shot. As I located my target, I remembered a quote from the movie called *The Patriot* starring Mel Gibson. "Aim small, miss small...your life depends on this," he told his young boys right before they went into battle.

I locked into my target, and a without a single blink slowly walked towards my ball. *Lock, Walk, Waggle Relax...* my inner voice repeated as my eyes remained constant on the target like a laser. I had practiced locking onto my target and ball awareness the entire week leading into this event. Confidently, I walked towards my ball and didn't look down until the last second. Completely locked in, I gave it a couple of waggles, one look back at my target, back to the ball, and then BOOM. I hit the ball dead on my line as it disappeared into the shadow in front of the green. "Great shot!" one of the guys on the tee proclaimed.

I jumped in the official cart and gratefully caught a ride towards the green. Sam met me near the path walking my putter in hand. I could see my ball on the surface 35 feet from the hole. "Nice job *Double A* remember to *Putt to your Picture*," Sam reminded me under his breath.

The Buddha watching intently and just before I hit the putt in my dream, turned my direction and stated, "Why do you think you were able to roll in that putt for par?" Realizing we were still in the dream, *but it felt so real,* I responded, "Because... I am the man?" I jokingly stated.

The Buddha clearly didn't respond to my humor. He remained stoic and continued to explain, "By letting go of outcomes, attachments, and desires you were able to overcome the lost ball and remain detached." I laughed, "I wasn't *that* attached to that ball anyway." I sensed the Buddha found humor in my comment, or so I believed. He further clarified that he was often misquoted saying, "Attachment is the root cause of suffering." He clarified that what he actually said was, "*Excessive* attachment was the root cause." One can want to make the putt, but not be excessively attached to the outcome."

"The **First Noble Truth** is often translated as "Life is suffering." This is another misquotation. If in life there was only suffering than there wouldn't be times of joy, sweetness, and ecstasy. *Logic* would dictate that it was a misquotation. What I said was "*In* life, there is suffering," Just like in your golf game," he clarified. I could swear there was a little tonal inflection in the ribbing of my golf game at the end of his sentence. I loved how the Buddha would catch me completely off guard and throw in a little humor occasionally.

He saw that I correctly made the distinctions in my mind, as his communication was clear and comforting. Catching me off guard again with a little humor, he quipped, "at last you understand a very secret Buddhist term *Parfection!* Knowing that he was just kidding with me, I laughed so hard, I nearly fell out of the *Buddha Balcony.* While his external demeanor didn't change, he had to be laughing inside. I was in awe of his comedic timing.

We returned just as the ocean goer of a par putt rolled in, dead center, and dropped to the bottom of the cup. The scene began to slowly fade away...

Impatiently I looked over at the Buddha and said, "What the heck? That was just getting good. I ended up shooting the course record and beat some really good players in the process," I continued. "Tiger, Phil, and VJ played the Western Open that year just to name a few."

The Buddha retorted, "Andrew, this is your ego speaking. Must I show you again how you lived in your past? Your efforting to find some form of confidence or self-worth is obstructing your game, your life and your *Buddha Nature.* Allowing your ego this use of the past will only create more suffering." As I remained on the *Buddha Balcony,* I anticipated the Buddha had more to show me, then another scene appeared.

Whoosh... I could see Sam Sarazen carrying my sometimes overly heavy Staff bag down the fairway. Sam hated that I had that heavy eyesore of a Staff bag and would strip it down to bare bones including rain gear unless clouds were prevalent. One time he even took off my club member bag tag because it had metal on it.

"Can't you find anything smaller or lighter?" Sam would always complain. I constantly reminded him that a smaller lighter bag had zero room for a paying sponsor logo, which is how I could afford him as my caddie.

I continued watching and began to recognize the location. The scene was of the tough 15th hole at Fort Ord- Bayonet course, in beautiful Seaside, California. This was the site of the ***05' Qualifying School Second Stage*** and the sight of my own personal golf tragedy. I followed myself up the hill to the 15th tee and remembered feeling the wind at my back, thinking: *I might need a 3 wood. Unfortunately, Sam was already 250 yards down the fairway.*

I remember deciding to take a line farther left than was comfortable since hitting driver straight down the fairway would cause the ball to go into the bunker at the end of the dog-leg left. The strike felt like a 1.50 smash factor on the Trackman as I sent the drive up over the corner of the dog-leg. Since I couldn't see the ball hit the ground, I looked directly at Sam in the tree line to see his reaction. As I saw his head drop, he looked back at the tee, and it was obvious that I had driven it too far, through the fairway. *Had I hit it too well? Was that even possible?* I remember thinking.

As I approached the location where the ball had ended, I was completely stymied behind the cart shed along the thick Cypress tree line. As if this hole wasn't hard enough, I had left myself with no-shot to one of the toughest greens on the course. "Give me the 5 iron," I growled. I proceed to punch the ball low under the trees and back into play. Leaving myself with 125 yards to the hole, I went with a pitching wedge. I flushed the ball dead center, and it flew two feet from the cup as I watched in disbelief as my ball zipped all the way to the front edge of the green. "Wow, I suck," I uttered under my breath. Trying to calm me down, Sam looked at me and said, "Relax Pro... you got this."

I witnessed the confidence Sam had in me as we watched his interaction with my younger self. As we continued to watch I knew damn well what the outcome would be, a 3 putt from 75 feet and a double bogie!

"Fuck!" I exploded. Sam looked over at me and said, "Ten seconds Pro." Sam knew I was hotter than hell and quickly reminded me that we had agreed upon ten seconds as the maximum time to complain about a previous shot and to detach from the outcome like it was an ex-girlfriend.

I would end my complaining by taking that red-ass to the 16th and ripping a perfect fade against the Cypress lined, right to the left-leaning fairway. In the perfect position, I hammered down on a full 48-degree Vockey pitching wedge to 12' from the cup. "I really need to make this putt," I said to Sam. "I had this putt in the practice round, it's pretty straight up the hill." I didn't take much time and buried it center cut.

As we approached the 17th tee I thought, *my entire golfing career had built up to this very moment.* I stood on the tee of the 71st hole, 2nd stage of PGA *Tour School*, needing a couple of pars to get a Tour Card.

I remember being in-between clubs. The wind that had been at my back earlier on 15 was now off my left, and the pin was also on the left, making this shot even tougher. I had decided to hit a ¾ punch 6 iron instead of the full 7 iron to keep it under the wind. As I sat behind myself, I cringed while I watched as I knew the result- a semi-shank over the 50-foot-high fence onto the range—a 2 shot penalty. I proceeded to hit a provisional with a 7 iron and knock it on the green and would two-putt for another double bogey.

The Buddha again waved his hand in front of me as we changed scenes. "Do you remember this moment?" the Buddha asked. As I focused in and the picture became clear I responded, "I do, in fact. That day was unforgettable." I was fortunate enough to caddie for Hall-of-Famer Lee Trevino and his guest Lawrence Welk's Grandson, Kevin, in the Member-Guest at Bighorn Golf Club.

On the 8th Hole, Kevin was in-between clubs. He turned towards Lee and said, "Hey Lee, do you like the 8 or the 9 iron from here?"

Mr. Trevino, who is one of the greatest to ever strike a golf ball questioned back, "Does your last name end in O?" Kevin looked confused… "HUH?" Lee continued, "I'm not talking Trevin-O…. I'm talking P R O." "If you are not a PRO, you need to hit a full shot with a full swing. Swing hard, be aggressive, and most importantly stay in balance."

I looked over at the Buddha and smiled, "I sure could have used this tip at Bayonet in '05!"

The Buddha waved his hand again... Whoosh. We had returned to the 18th tee at Bayonet. I could see from the *Buddha Balcony* that I was hotter than the barrel of a pistol. For a moment I even thought I saw smoke coming off me.

I remember my mind was wandering as I slowly made my way up the hill to the 18th. My head was down, but my focus still on having butchered the previous holes. My energy was being driven in the wrong direction, and my mind was full of negative thoughts. After driving into the left tree line on a par 5, reachable with a long iron for me, I was forced to lay-up to yardage and try and get up and down from there. I hit a nice lay-up and spun a Vokey 56-degree sand wedge from 96 yards to 14 feet.

Approaching the green, I had finally calmed down and realized the opportunity in front of me as I circled the hole like a tiger on the prowl. I knew deep down in my heart that this putt had to drop. I put a nice stroke on the 14-footer. As the ball rolled towards the hole on a great line, stopping ¼ revolution short of going in for a birdie. It was so close I mean you couldn't stick a tee in the ground between the hole and the ball.

Once again, I missed by a single shot, finishing in 21st place with 20 players advancing. "That's right," I snarled at the Buddha, "I finished in 21st place all by myself, unheard of."

The Buddha nodded his head as if to say he understood my pain. Whoosh. The image of my idol Jack Sherpa appeared as if I was watching a giant television. He was being interviewed after winning that week. "Go with your question," Jack pointed to the reporter in the front.

"Mr. Sherpa, how do you always seem to avoid negative outcomes and win so often?" Jack grinned with pleasure as he started to explain. *"Well... growing up I worked very hard to become a really nice ball striker... from that point, I just needed to learn how to play the game and score better."* Jack continued by saying, *"I finally realized that golf is a game of misses, not always about your good shots, but rather how well you manage your poor ones."* Jack also expressed, *"Not all good shots end up good, but that doesn't make it a bad shot."*

Jack paused as he looked around the room. *"Haven't you ever hit a bad shot that ended up close to the hole or a great shot that ended worse than an ugly one? I know I have."* Jack smiled as he stood up and concluded the interview.

I thought about the message the Buddha presented before me. *Life isn't about being perfect but rather about how we treat or deal with our misses and mishaps in life. This was the secret Buddhist term of* *parfection,* I thought to myself. The Buddha's facial expression again didn't change, he just nodded with approval.

Home on the Range

Just when I thought I could finally start to see a slight smile on the Buddha's face, we flashed to my home. Our home was a place I cherished and loved. It was directly across the street from the only illuminated night range and the best 18-hole par 3 course in town. We frequented the range often, so we were a very well-known family by all the pros at the course. However, this was not what was reflected in what we were seeing from the *Buddha Balcony.*

With a pissed off look on my face, I was speaking quite loudly at the dogs for peeing on the side of my Club Glove Golf Travel Bag. "Which one of you did this to my Club Glove?" I screamed out as if the dogs could understand. "Seriously, I don't need this right now!" I barked on. I could see the scared look on the kids' faces as if they might be next. They had accidentally let the dogs in mid-day, and nobody had kept an eye on them.

I remember expressing my displeasure earlier that morning at everyone in the house for not cleaning up and that we lived in a five-bedroom house that didn't clean itself and that if we let dogs into the house, they must be watched. My blood pressure was rising as I watched my interactions. The *Buddha Balcony* was clearly becoming an emotional experience laboratory. I was learning that these lower emotions were blocking my golf abilities and my *Buddha Nature.*

It's been said that opposites attract, and I was lucky that my sweet wife Arya was the calm one us. To pacify me, rather than getting the kids to do it and risk that it was done poorly, she calmly cleaned up the mess. She defended everyone in the process and reminded me, "They are just dogs." Our ensuing verbal dispute would lead to door slamming and cussing, mostly by me of course. It was obvious I was feeling the pressure of life and would get angry at the smallest things. I was even getting angry that she wasn't using this as a teaching moment for the kids.

Looking over at the Buddha after seeing this scene, I could swear it made even his all-loving heart ache a little. I know my heart was aching as I watched. My actions were deplorable. I was not proud of myself.

While in the kitchen prepping for dinner Arya began projecting, "You know they are all afraid of you." "They aren't afraid of me," I retorted. As the family sat down for dinner, the silence was unsettling. I attempted to make conversation and get each person to talk about their day. "So, how was everyone's day?" Their responses were very generic and very singular. Answers were like, "Good," "Ok," "Don't know." Their lack of conversation engaged my internal dialogue, and it wanted to go practice. "I'm going to the practice range for a bit," I said to Arya. "I will be back in about an hour," I said dismissively. Not wanting anything to prevent my escape, I aggressively shut the door behind me.

The range was a great place to go to unwind, throw in my Air Pods, and get a little me time. I worked diligently on my basic alignment and ball position, knowing quality over quantity was essential to productive practice. While yogis in the Himalayas practiced withdrawing to a cave, this was my way to retreat. My swings of the club were my spiritual practice.

It was clear that the Buddha was eventually going to teach me some sort of meditation or mindfulness technique. *Who would have thought that my hole-in-one-ness was putting me on the path to holiness?*

By the time I returned from my evening range session, I was calmer. Arya had already put the kids to bed. We reconvened to continue the earlier conversation in the privacy of our bedroom. While quietly taking off my spike-less golf shoes, out of nowhere Arya appeared and reignited the spat earlier.

"I just don't understand your outbursts. You really scare the kids, the animals and me for that matter." Arya continued for a few minutes as I listened without saying a word until she was finished. I wasn't about to try and dignify my verbal out-lashing and quickly apologized for my previous actions. "I am sorry My Love," I repented. "I realize I am a very lucky man. You are my best friend."

I knew we could easily get past a few arguments because we truly loved each other and the kids. This heated argument, like many in the past, would end lovingly; however, my earlier behavior was unjust and needed to be rectified. As we brushed our teeth I gazed over at Arya until I caught her attention, "I love you," I whispered. "I love you more," she whispered back. Exhausted from our day it didn't take long as we snuggled up to each other before we were both counting sheep.

The Buddha's lips were always slightly smiling, and his composure was always highly content and peaceful. While his lips, barely moved, he was smiling more after watching this scene, at least by my perception. "You have a choice to mentally start your day -3 under par if you want. It's totally up to you," the Buddha expressed. I smiled from his synergy of ancient wisdom with golf lingo.

The history review invigorated me as if someone had given me a shot of a 5-hour energy drink. It was a blur of cognitive function identical to a computer searching for several files at once. I started to wonder, *how I could do better? Better with not judging others, better with my composure, better with managing my anger, better with the way I treated the kids and animals, and better with my golf game.* I also began to think; *maybe I could stop using substances like THC and alcohol.*

Could this be the road to a better life and a better golf game? Was this the answer to feeling better about my golf course life as well as my life's course, instead of *continually creating challenges for myself and being angry at the ones who loved me the most?* I was now desperate to find a solution and to get back on the road to success without suffering. The good news, as it appeared, was that I didn't have to come up with these answers myself. Someone far wiser was going to help me get there.

Good Morning!

Ouch… My head was heavy like a brick tied to the top of my noggin. I no longer on the beautiful *Buddha Balcony*, I felt the weight of being back in my physical body. I woke up wasn't -3 under par mentally, I was more like 3 over par as my head pounded.

I had fallen asleep with my head resting on a toilet paper roll on the drunk tank floor. My left arm was asleep from lying on it, and my temples felt like I had just shot 80.

I thought, *whoever designed these in-processing tanks was not thinking about human comfort.* There were no beds, and the only seat was the completely open, door-less shitter that was hanging on the wall. *It was guaranteed I wouldn't be taking a dump there—Period.*

My inner dialogue was interrupted by the loud scraping of the 4" thick solid steel door being unlocked. The desk sergeant announced my name, "Andrew Arleau, you've been bailed out."

As I approached the desk, my personal belongings were being dumped out of a manila envelope onto the counter. My favorite *Glacier Ice Polarized* sunglasses by Shady Rays were, of course, broken; probably due to this Jailer-Asshole's carelessness. I thought to myself, *at least they replace two free pairs a year, unlike other expensive brands.* I was trying to think of something positive on this most dismal of mornings.

One thing was for sure, I didn't see Sam's $1,000 in my money clip. "Sign this, here, here, and here," snapped the sergeant. I looked up at the clock directly behind Sergeant Ramirez, "6:29 AM--Is that correct?" I softly asked. "You bet your drunk driving ass it's correct." The other officer behind the out-processing counter was now looking over at me, "How was your little nap?" he chirped with a condescending tone. I wasn't sure what to say, so I kept my mouth shut.

It seemed like hours had elapsed, yet it had only been 40 minutes. Barely coherent and still stunned from the early morning events, all I could focus on was getting out of this place immediately.

After being guided through a secure area and eventually to the front door, I had never felt so excited to be outside. Arya greeted me by jumping into my arms and giving me a massive hug and kiss. She was parked directly outside the main doors, so we quickly jumped into our other vehicle and headed home.

During the drive home I was coming into my waking consciousness. I started reflecting and asked myself if I had really had a dream with a Golden Buddha. *I did feel very different*. I was far more refreshed than any 40-minute power nap I had ever taken. Despite not knowing what was going to happen I felt I could cope. I believed somehow everything was going to be okay.

Then it dawned on me. While I had learned a lot about my issues, I had also witnessed many examples of how I needed to proceed in order to improve. I didn't get a chance to learn about the **Three Priceless or Precious Techniques** that the Buddha alluded to. I couldn't even remember what they were called, and I wondered what I was going to do.

After arriving home, Arya attentively made me a bowl of chicken noodle soup and a grilled cheese which filled the empty pit in my stomach. She suggested I take a shower and get some rest. My cognitive and emotional processors were still a little fragile. I allowed Arya's loving kindness to ease me back into the comfort of home. The kids all still asleep, never noticed that I hadn't come home, let alone had just arrived.

Arya had called a friend within the Sheriff's Department and reassured me that all would be okay and that nobody had been hurt in the accident. That was great news and I could feel some tension release from my body. My feet felt heavy along with and my stiff neck and sore body as I lumbered up the stairs. It felt as if I was wearing golf shoes and the cleats were caught in the shag carpet. After trudging up the stairs, I quickly collapsed onto the bed with my clothes still on.

The Three Priceless Techniques Dream

Exhausted from riding the emotional roller coaster of the day, my body fell asleep once it flopped down onto my Lady Americana Celebrity Mattress. It seemed like only minutes until suddenly I heard a whisper in my head. "Andrew, the life you wished for while in the jail cell is *possible; it does exist!"* the Buddha said. "The world of *Maya* that you are living in is an illusion. It is merely an illusion within your mind."

The Buddha was sitting Indian style, patiently hovering in the air in my dream. While his exterior was one of calmness, I intuited he was excited to share new revelations, I was relieved and excited that he was back. His radiance showered me with a euphoria of sorts, better than anything I had ever experienced. It was clear to me that I needed to learn something more to put an end to the misery of what my mind had created in my life and for those around me.

While in my dream state, I was conversing with the Buddha doing reviews of my past and began to recognize the thinking that created my life. It was almost as If everything was a dream, or rather, as the Buddha said, *"Maya,* an illusion." I remembered that before we had reviewed my day, I asked the magic question, "How can I change the illusion?"

The ever-perceptive Buddha smiled and said, "Now, I will teach you the **Three Priceless Techniques** that will transform your illusion and thus your suffering.

Before I teach you the **First Priceless Technique,** what do you see when you look at yourself?"

In Planck time, the smallest increment, or roughly 10^-44 second, a mirror appeared on the *Buddha Balcony.* The Buddha motioned for me to look and compassionately asked me "What do you see?"

I looked at myself and saw a man who was tired, losing his hair and the virility of his youth, who had bags under his eyes, and wrinkles on his forehead. I decided to sum up my current existence by answering the Buddha with, "I see a tired golfer."

He replied, "The **First Priceless Technique** is that you need to remember, you are a Buddha and that you have a *Buddha Nature."* When he spoke, his tone had a most unique quality—it was not demeaning or condescending—it contained deep truth, sprinkled with unconditional love and acceptance.

"I am a Buddha? What does this mean?" I queried.

The Buddha poetically paused for a moment and said softly with a tinge of excitement, "It means you are awake! You are seeing past the dream. In other words, you are living *outside* this world of physical illusion. A Buddha no longer experiences the anguish, misery, and suffering that you experienced in your reviews. A Buddha is filled with a tranquil abiding, deep peace, empathy, and compassion. When you thought you were having a reaction to events that were occurring in the *Buddha Balcony,* they were actually just your projections." I chuckled to myself and quickly realized I needed to stay on task.

He further lovingly explained, "Unfortunately Andrew, you are blocking your true *Buddha Nature,* since you are identifying yourself with *Maya,* the world of illusion. You see, the physical world that you currently live in, and all the thoughts and emotions that go along with it, are merely illusions. If you break down the word enlightenment, it literally means *to lighten the mind (and the emotions).* You do this by removing the heaviness caused by your negative emotions and thoughts."

Wow! I thought *this is how people must feel after taking a golf lesson.* For a second, I began to wonder if I would be able to understand these techniques, much less implement them into my life and in golf. I didn't even know what tranquil abiding meant. Although being filled with deep peace was enticing, it also sounded unrealistic. "How do I change that?' I inquired.

"It's really quite simple," answered the Buddha. "Close your eyes, put your tongue on the roof of your palate, and imagine that you are a Golden Buddha of pure bright golden light. Then imagine that a rainbow of light is emanating in concentric circles all around you. Continue to imagine these concentric circles of rainbow light growing outward and towards infinity and see yourself becoming an ever-expanding Golden Buddha."

If my physical lips were moving or not, I couldn't tell. In this dream, I felt like I was grinning from ear to ear as I started applying this **Technique.** My body felt lighter and my stress was rapidly dissipating. It was like snow melting from the heat radiating from the sun. I was in awe of how fast the **First Priceless Technique** was working. I was experiencing deeper levels of peace with each passing moment. Physically, my shoulders had sunk deep into the bed. My breathing became deeper, yet slower, and my face felt like it was glowing. *WOW!* I thought to myself, *this is amazing!*

"Andrew, the result of this **Technique** is to bring about your true nature--your *Buddha Nature.* Your physical body is like the tip of an inverted iceberg. Invisibly your spiritual energy bodies emanate upward and outward in all directions, the Buddha elucidated.

Now I will show you an Advanced Version of this **Technique.** This version will be applicable if you are under stress or not feeling much like your true *Buddha-Self.* Please visualize a Golden Buddha descending from the heavens, or what Buddhists call *Tushita.* Visualize the Golden Buddha coming down *through* the top of your head." The Buddha paused for a moment as he watched me comprehend and simulate this initial part of the **Technique. "**As you bring down the Golden Buddha through the top of your head and into your body, you merge the Buddha into you and you into it. From the center of your heart, you then visualize rainbow concentric circles of light spiraling outward in all ten directions. Merging with the Buddha at the beginning is vital to the **Technique's** success because it helps bring about the tranquil and empowering energy of the Buddha which helps to cultivate your Buddhahood. The concentric rings of light emerging from the heart help transform the environment around you."

He sagaciously paused for a moment. My mind was again like an iPod shuffle looking to queue my favorite music. I realized that by identifying myself as *just a golfer,* I was limiting myself. I was seeing only the tip of the iceberg and into what was really my true existence. To test this new **Technique**, I imagined myself dressed like a golfer and identified as one, standing on the *Buddha Balcony.* Momentarily, I was proud of myself for leading the experience, almost like I was learning to fly and gaining lift. The image was very faint as if I couldn't maintain the connection. It was starting to become painful and difficult to focus on. I was started to feel pressure in my head and had trouble breathing. My body felt weak and heavy. "Whew! I said, "Enough of that!"

I changed the image on the *Buddha Balcony Mirror* to a picture of myself as a Buddha. *Ahhhh...* resoundingly went off in my inner ears. I could feel the peace in my mind, body, and soul. The Buddha was right. Being a Buddha was far better than just being a golfer. The image disappeared as I turned back to the Buddha.

The Buddha said it was time for learning **Priceless Technique Number Two**.

"Andrew, when you look at your world what do you see?" he asked.

I immediately thought of the review where I saw my tired body, tired mind, and all the sadness and conflict. It appeared turmoil had surrounded me over the years. I said, "My world is full of conflict. It is a pretty dark place."

The Golden Buddha paused. He gently and sweetly confirmed, "You are correct." The world as you currently see it (from your *Andrew perspective)* is full of excessive attachment, ignorance, conflict, turmoil, sadness, and thus suffering. While *yes* there are times of happiness and success, these times are waning, and later suffering is inevitable. Buddhists call this world of suffering *Samsara. Samsara* is the cycle of death and rebirth to which one's life in the material world is bound. As you learn to see the world through your *Buddha Nature,* you will see past the world of form and illusion that is plaguing you and others.

"Andrew, since you are a Buddha, you must remember that the location you are in, wherever you are, is a *Buddha Field*. The energy that radiates from your Buddha presence inherently can help transform the environment around you into a *Buddha Field*," he clarified. "**Priceless Technique Number Two** is seeing the environment around you, and the world in general, as a *Buddha Field.* You see past the illusion and see the environment as pure radiant light. It is like the way that you see yourself as a Buddha, which is a limitless view of yourself. Yes, there is darkness in the world, but you can help to transform it into light," he wisely concluded.

Pondering myself as a Buddha was a big mental leap. In my life game, it was like jumping up two new levels and earning a free upgrade. The idea that I could be influencing my locale was equivalent to moving from a Two Terabyte system to a 93 Petaflop, which can perform 93,000 trillion calculations per second.

Curiously, I closed my eyes and imagined the world around me transforming into a *Buddha Field.* Feeling an even greater peace, it now dawned on me that peace had levels. My inner mind chatter began to slow, then stopped, or rather just went silent.

My mind chatter was now gone--well almost gone--as my old inner dialogue chose to fight back. Competing with the vacuum, my mind started to fill up again with chatter. Attempting to preserve itself, the inner voices started talking about my mind's lack of talking. It was almost humorous.

In the interplay of voice versus silence, with silence winning, my breath and tempo started slowing. As silence emerged victoriously, I experienced a profound feeling of love that I had never known before. It was deeper than the love I felt when I held my newborn child for the very first time. The sweetness was sublime. I was in a total state of bliss!

With these profound changes, I noticed my mind and emotions had corresponding effects on my physical body. As my mind became clearer in thought and quicker in response, my physical eyes showed brighter. The congestion in my lungs and sinuses started clearing up, and the underlying tension in my neck and upper back loosened. As my new-found bliss started increasing, my breathing repetition slowed, and the tension in my chest released. It seemed there was a relationship between this release of anxious tension and the slowing of my heartbeat.

This was a welcomed relief from my hypertension and my lack of patience, from which I had suffered from for years after my *Pushing Tin* days at the ATC job. I felt my blood pressure normalizing along with my breathing pattern easing. I started entertaining the possibility of a day that I might no longer need weed and alcohol to relax at night. The process was like being in a virtual spa. I was working out the tightness in my body as the serenity of this healing space melted my tension away.

I shared with the Buddha that the people around me in my imaginary *Buddha Field* were all dressed in saffron robes, glowing and smiling. I could feel an electrical buzz in the air, like waves of energy. I wondered, c*ould this be what a woman might experience with a vibrator? If it was anything close to this--it is was pretty awesome!!!* My new level of consciousness seemed to enable me to feel deeper levels of peace, stillness and now ecstasy.

The Buddha oddly leaned towards me and asked, "Andrew, do you know why Tiger Woods always wears a red shirt and black pants on Sunday?" I looked at the Buddha completely shocked by his question. I shyly smiled, yet I already knew the answer because Gina Coffman had let me in on the secret years ago. I responded, "To make Tiger's decision making simple on Sundays and to detach himself from materialism?" The Buddha nodded in agreement.

"Very good, Andrew, you are a quick learner," the Buddha confidently praised as he continued. "It was not only to symbolize Tiger's own simplicity but to make it simple for his followers and fans. As sure as the sun will come up, everyone knows Tiger will show up in a red shirt, black pants and sporting his trademark black cap on Sunday."

"I love it!" I quickly interjected as I continued listening to the Buddha. I was waiting for him to unveil **Priceless Technique Number Three.**

"Now that you've experienced your *Buddha Nature*-- your true nature, Andrew-- it is very easy to imagine that you're a Buddha. It is very easy to imagine that all around you is a *Buddha Field.* Over time, and with practice, you will not have to work at this process. It will become easier, and you will be transformed into this natural state," he articulated.

Similar to how I tested the concepts I learned with **Priceless Technique Number One**, I imagined looking at the world from my normal *Andrew perspective*. *Talk about a crash and burn.* I literally felt like I was dropped from the heavens into a deep crevasse when I looked at the world through this

Samsaric lens. The world looked even darker than before and the people that I worked with looked *ghoulish*.

My thoughts quickly reverted to my *Buddha World,* or what was now known in my new vernacular as a *Buddha Field.* Instead of seeing just the conflicts and alike, I now saw the people as Souls. I got a glimpse of how these conflicts darkened their Souls—as if the conflicts surrounded them with hideous energies. It was a little scary, but I now understood why people were literally chained to *Samsara* without this *Buddha Vision.*

The Buddha observed that I was getting a little weirded out by this new revelation. Seeing the true nature of others was shocking, but I think he knew I could handle it. It was probably best that I realized how I was on the path to being tethered to *Samsara.* Seeing this new reality would provide motivation to get out.

The Buddha reached up and hit the pause button and patiently asked, "Are you ready for **Priceless Technique Number Three**?"

I got the feeling, by the way, he said it that this **Technique** was going to be a great deal harder. The first two were pretty easy, so I thought *there must be some sort of catch with the* ***Third.***

Will I have to make one hundred, four-foot putts in a row, every other one with my eyes closed? Maybe hit balls off one leg for 3 hours in a G-string? I snickered, wondering what it could be, exuberant and slightly apprehensive, "Yes, please share it with me," I enthusiastically replied.

"As I said," the Buddha continued, "The first **Two Techniques** are very easy to apply. The third is also easy; however, most people will find it difficult to apply at first. With practice, this technique will be the most rewarding for you, and it can also help others even more, as well!"

"Andrew, imagine seeing someone that you love," he said. I immediately imagined my wife, Arya. *She is so sexy and smart,* I thought, as my teeth peeked out from behind my lips. The Buddha could see me smiling. "Andrew, now imagine someone you don't like," he countered with. I imagined one of my fellow tour players whom we called *The Cheater,* Charlie Yama. I could picture his face and imagined his annoying fake laugh.

I started to hear his bragging voice... "Nobody can beat me at home!" I was just about to tell the Buddha about Charlie's reputation for cheating when the Buddha wisely interrupted with, "What is the difference in how you see these people?"

I had never really thought about it. The way I saw others popped into my head. It just seemed normal to judge others. I thought for a moment and replied, "When I see Arya, I'm focused on her good qualities, but when my golfing opponents appear their negative qualities stick out like a sore thumb," I replied.

The Buddha started a new declaration, **"**As you learned in the first **Two Priceless Techniques** the world you are living in is an illusion, like a dream world of your ordinary perceptions. The physical world is an illusion, and the real world is a world of energy. You now have a greater understanding of that reality from when you turned into a Buddha and experienced the world as a *Buddha Field."*

"So, recapping," the Buddha said, "since you are a Buddha, having a *Buddha Nature*, you would never harm anyone or anything. There is a Buddhist principle called *ahimsa,* which means non-injury. By applying this **Third Technique**, you certainly wouldn't hurt anyone physically, nor would you hurt anyone with your mind (your thoughts) or speech."

"When you were annoyed with other players, caddies, or even volunteers for moving or playing slowly; When you were frustrated with your own poor play and judged your Pro-Am partners as hackers and choppers; When your kids annoy you at home or your wife was in your ear--All these judgments and emotions were emanating from your *non-Buddha-Nature*. To make matters worse, negative perceptions towards these people project negative energy at them. Like the return of a boomerang, these hurtful energies rebound onto your *Buddha Nature*. Everyone gets hurt in the process.

In his hand, the Buddha was now holding chains and shackles. He said, "These interactions further chain you to Samsara—**chaining you to perpetual suffering**.

It is my karma to share this with information with you. It is your karma as to what you do with it. In a Planck moment of time, the chains and shackles disappeared. *I hope I could fully learn this lesson in as fast a time.*

He paused for a moment to let the message sink in. The depth of his words touched my heart, and in fact, the depths of my Soul. The Buddha's loving yet firm message awakened me. The Buddha was right. I would never intentionally harm someone, yet I had been. I never considered harming anyone with a thought.

"Each person whether you chose to like them or not, is just like you. They are just people on their way to reaching their *Buddha Nature.* Some are farther down the road than others; many are rookies and have just started practicing. This is **Priceless Technique Number Three,** and you must remember that others are Buddhas and to see them as such," he concluded.

For the first time in my dreams with the Buddha, I was a little disenchanted. I felt some apprehension as to whether I could actually apply this last **Technique.** "It was kind of like the last time I made 9 birdies in the first 14 holes, totally *in the so-called zone,* then out of nowhere someone in the group blurted out, "He, could break the course record."

Astonished at the loud comment, I was abruptly pulled out of my "don't think of the score" (in the zone) state. I had been thinking, *most definitely I'll bury my ball in the bunker on the 15th hole, AND I'll follow that with a 3 putt.* I felt my consciousness and energy contract as negativity flooded my body as the egoic consciousness kicked in after the vocal interruption.

With profound wisdom and compassion, the Buddha obviously sensed I was slightly confused, suggesting that I simply, "Give it a try it's surprisingly easy after a little practice. It is just like how you mastered your Grip technique."

He said, "Imagine yourself, and a few other players close by on the range, working with your coach as he compliments you in front of everyone." I began to visualize the moment in my head. "Andrew you sure have been playing well!" Coach stated as he continued, "You've been driving the golf ball very well today." Immediately we reappeared on the *Buddha Balcony* to watch the scene play out. As soon as Coach complimented me, I saw dirty red energy from a few people nearby start to ooze its way towards me. *I had seen their negative thoughts and how they were affecting me!*

Next, I got to learn indifference. Coach replaced the positive affirmations with quiet comments under his breath that nobody else could hear. "All that aside, you may want to work on your wedge game, based on the stats I have seen." In praise or in criticism, my emotions remained stable, and my sense of peacefulness didn't waver; thus I was on the path to learning indifference.

The Buddha's simplicity of his words put me at ease. His radiance was something to behold. With a new-found sense of compassion for my detractors, I considered how my fellow players might have help feelings of jealousy. They only heard the beginning of the conversation and not the second half with the criticism. Although they didn't outwardly show it, nonetheless they had an envious vibe. "Ok, I totally follow now," I said to the Buddha.

Able to see and feel this envy energy in my dream, the Buddha stated, "The world of energy is more real than the physical realm." As I recalled his words, I had a clearer understanding.

I loved being on the *Buddha Balcony* as it brought out my *Buddha Intelligence.* I was able to easily put new concepts together. I reflected on expressions that we use daily and how the colors in these idioms reflect energy. *Green with envy* meant jealousy. *Feeling blue today* denoted sadness. *A yellow-belly* reflected someone who was afraid. *My ears are burning* (red) demonstrated dirty, red energy had been by others. *Whoa! I loved these realizations!*

It now dawned on me that as a Buddha I could have access to omniscience, as well. I thought I detected the Buddha smiling *at yet another realization* as he said, "Let us continue..."

The Buddha told me to once again, "Imagine yourself becoming a Buddha of pure golden light with rainbow light emanating and then to see the driving range and the 1st Tee as a *Buddha Field.* Now, you can call it a *Buddha Fairway.* Imagine it lined with beautiful lotus flowers." I visualized it, and it *was bodacious!* *I amused myself at the similarities in the words bodacious and Buddhacious!*

The Buddha also suggested, "Re-imagine playing partners and other caddies and turn them into Buddhas of pure light by applying **Priceless Technique Number Three**." With a bit of apprehension, I began to feel incredible lightness. Then I felt bliss taking me even higher than I had ever felt earlier in the dream. *The Buddha was right- it was Buddhaful!* I gleefully said to myself. *This* ***Priceless Technique*** *was the Crown Jewel of the* ***Three!***

In this moment of reflection, I realized a profound similarity. That of embodying a Buddha and seeing others as pure golden light. I remember the word enlightenment meant making the mind light rather than entangled with gray, dirty, heavy energy. *Light felt good,* I deduced.

I automatically smiled as my lips seemed to move on their own accord. I hadn't ever realized until now just how much stress I had previously carried in my facial muscles, let alone the rest of my body. There are 50 muscles in the face, and many are rarely used. With most people carrying so much tension, these latent muscles just atrophy set in. It seemed as I became lighter, it was easier to want to stay that way.

"How many people know about these **Three Priceless Techniques**?" I asked.

"Not enough," wittily yet profoundly replied the Buddha.

The Buddha, in all his omniscience, also possessed humor, timing, and wit. I also felt great compassion emanating from the Buddha. Before, I thought it was sadness, but now I realized it to be compassion. I sensed how much he wanted others to know these **Techniques.** I also saw in his body language, that he wanted people to stop ignorantly hurting each other with their words, thoughts, and deeds. Although these were just my projections, these realizations gave me a boost of energy, confidence, and a purpose. I felt like I was a part of something much bigger than myself.

"Well," I said, "how many people would be enough?"

"Great question!" the Buddha fired back. "There are approximately seven billion people in the physical world on earth. If seven million or more applied the **Three Priceless Techniques**, it would create a tsunami wave of positive energy. If done simultaneously and consistently it could transform the physical world into a *Buddha Field...forever*."

The Buddha further explained that when a person becomes a Buddha, their energy field (invisible, spiritual bodies) expands more than ten times. As they create a *Buddha Field,* the frequency of that location is also purified and multiplied by still another ten-fold. He alluded to speaking more about the group application of these **Priceless Techniques** at another time and how it dramatically multiplied everything.

I mentally did the math. *By starting with 7,000,000 people (or roughly 1/10th of 1% percent of the population), multiplying their energy 10 times by applying* ***Priceless Technique Number One,*** *then multiplying the energy of their location 10 times by applying* ***Priceless Technique Number Two,*** *and lastly multiplying the energy of others around them by 10 (by seeing them as Buddhas) as in* ***Priceless Technique Number Three****, this profound equation results in 7,000,000,000 transformed sentient beings. The magnitude of the wave of Buddha Fields from this equation could be enough to help all seven billion people.* The Buddha seemed to be smiling, even more, *I was on to something*. Internally I was inspired by my math skills and the opportunity to touch 1/10th of the 60 million golfers in the world.

A New Day

Wham! I slammed back into my body... My crash landing felt hard and heavy as I awakened back into the physical world. The clock read 5:44 as the early morning sun beamed directly into my eyes through the small crack in the curtain. The dew was running down the window on this brisk pre-winter morning. I woke up realizing the Buddha was gone, but the remnants of the Buddha's instruction remained. These seeds had been planted; however, seeds take time to germinate and develop into plants. *With these remnants, I was resolved to build my own Buddha within, and to transform my world into a Buddha Field (Fairway)!*

After Arya bailed me out and took me home, I fell into a state of animated suspension and slept for the next 24 hrs. Two days later, I still hadn't finished my DUI checklist, other than contacting our attorney, T. Lance Archer Esq., for an appointment. When we arrived at Lance's office, Arya and I both immediately knew that we were in good hands.

"Time to put all these issues aside and just focus on only the things in your control and let me handle the legal stuff," Lance stated as he paused to take a deep breath, "Guys, I got this." Lance firmly reassured us as he continued. "Don't you have a PGA *Tour School* this week?" Surprised that he had remembered, I responded, "Yes, it starts this Tuesday, and pre-training starts tomorrow." Lance gave me a confident pat on the back as he walked me out to the lobby, "You will be just fine, stay positive!"

With all the stress from the last couple of days of chaos, I was relieved *Tour School* was finally here. Eager to utilize **The Three Priceless Techniques** and poised to face the stresses of the tournament, I knew it was vital to put everything on the back burner for now, so to speak, and to begin preparing for the trip ahead.

My brother Ward was flying into Palm Springs International to caddie for me, and I would be picking him up in a few hours along the way to Goat Valley Country Club, host of this year's **PGA Champions Tour Regional Qualifying School.**

In preparation for the day, I started off right. I had been was lucky. A world renown anti-aging expert Dr. Nick Delgado had changed my life 20 years ago. Dr. Nick knew his stuff! He used to do live blood cell analysis for the participants at Tony Robbins events. He diagnosed my adrenals as depleted, probably due to all my years of stress, and said I was cortisol deficient. To help my current state, I popped several of his Adrenal DMGs. Dr. Nick was the best example that his cutting products and processes worked. He is still a stud in his mid-60s and a few years ago set a world record doing 1,993 vertical lifts over his head. Without stopping for an hour, he moved over 50,000 pounds that night. I was there for this Herculean feat, and to this day no one has come even close to his record.

Next, I jumped in my Infra-Red Sauna from www.JNHLifestyles.com. I loved doing it just before bed, as my muscles melted under the pleasant heat--making my slumber divine. There was no steam, no EMF radiation and it wasn't too hot inside. It was the perfect temperature inside and was also a perfect place for me to meditate.

After springing out of the sauna I felt extremely energetic and light, somewhere *slightly under par,* and I threw on my USAF sweatshirt, khakis, and my favorite Black Clover "Live Lucky" hat. I made my way for my usual pre-golf stretch and visualization session. Stretching had become a must, as my now 50-year-old body was tighter and more prone to injury. I diligently went thru my stretch routine as usual. My body felt almost on par and ready to play competitive golf, with one exception, my right shoulder and neck just didn't feel right. I reflected, *Did I reinjure myself?* Then it came to me. I had slept on a toilet paper roll, on a stone-cold floor, in a jail cell! That would probably knock anyone's shoulder out of whack.

"Arya!" I yelled down the hall from my training room. I heard her footsteps coming down the hall. "Yes, My Love?" Arya questioned, as she walked into the room. "My neck and right shoulder are super stiff and sore," I continued in a semi-panicked voice, "Any chance I could meet with Dr. Tom Iwashita over at Tamarisk Country Club before I head out of town today?" I grabbed my shoulder as I massaged my neck, "I could really use a neck and shoulder adjustment." Arya smiled and stated, "Let me make a call and find out!"

I had already planned with the Head Pro, Kyle Kelly aka *"2K"* to stop at Tamarisk C.C. and roll a few putts with my flex putter trainer, on their super slick putting surfaces, and to meet with Gina *Magic* Coffman for one last mental session.

Tamarisk C.C. is so known for its superfast greens that even PGA Tour Superstar Fred Couples dubbed Tamarisk "The Best Greens in the Desert" when they were still on the Bob Hope Desert Classic rotation. Developed in the early 50's it boasts a deep history of A-list celebrities and professionals. Ben Hogan was hired as the first head pro at Tamarisk, and it was the second 18 Hole private club ever built in the Coachella Valley. Tamarisk C.C. is also home to Frank Sinatra's compound.

I could hear Arya coming down the hallway. "So, I just got off the phone with 2K and Dr. Iwashita, and everything is a go." Arya continued, "Aren't you meeting Gina *Magic* as well? "Yes," I replied. "Well you better get going, or you'll be late picking up Ward at the Airport," as Arya shuffled me towards our bathroom.

I quickly jumped into the shower. The hot water warmed my sore, achy muscles and helped my backside stretch in the hope of visualizing greatness in my future. I closed my eyes as the water splashed off my throbbing shoulder and neck. My mind suddenly, out of nowhere, was flooded by negative dialogue. I had dubbed this negative self-talking state *"Old Andrew."*

I growled under my breath, becoming more apoplectic by the minute. *Can't believe Sam skipped on the $1,000 I'd won from him.*

I began revisiting conversations from months ago from the 19th hole. Anyone with a golf opinion eagerly and continuously reminded me that there were "only five fully exempt cards available at the **Champions Tour Finals**." *Like I didn't already know that fact? I mean seriously, I was the guy paying the not so cheap, entry fee.* All this negativity made my shoulder and neck throb even more.

The steam from the shower finally warmed the rest of my *not-so-young-anymore body.* I remembered when I was a kid, I thought 30 was old but 50 was the new 30, and I felt pretty good, injuries aside. My newfound **Techniques** helped me shrug *"Old Andrew"* off. It now seemed as if the world of dreams and the real world were merging. It was both surreal and sublime.

With the most mental and emotional clarity I had ever experienced, I recounted the **Three Priceless Techniques:** *"Become a Buddha, check! Transform the surrounding area into a Buddha Field, check! And, most importantly, visualize everyone in that Buddha Field as a Golden Buddha of pure emanating rainbow light, check!"*

Before exiting the steamy shower, I had my full positive self back while I took on my Buddha countenance. The anticipation and stress of the day began to melt away, just like it had happened in the dream. My breathing was becoming freer, and my heartbeat had slowed. My shoulders began to relax.

These physical responses were confirmation that the **Techniques** were working.

Taking long, deep breaths, I further calmed myself as I reimagined my life with all its chaos and visualized my body as a Buddha sitting in a *Buddha Field* staring down a *Buddha Fairway* lined with bright magenta lotus flowers. I also envisioned my beautiful wife Arya and her wonderful children, each as young Buddhas. It was so easy to do since my love for them was so strong. I pictured everyone running over to hug me and love on me, projecting positive magnetic energy.

After exiting the shower, I rushed to pack as I prepared to leave. The positivity I had been feeling permeated the household and everyone was at peace. Watching this new, surreal *real* world with my own eyes brought a most gratifying smile to my face.

Arya had come out to the driveway just as I had finished packing our RV for the trip. The sun was rising just over her shoulder. She certainly appeared to embody a glowing Buddha! Our lips met as she embraced me with a squeeze like no other, I had felt in my life, as was if our energy fields had merged and sparked a giant beam of light. "I Love you," I whispered. "I love you more." she softly whispered back. The positive energy of the entire house seemed to also affect our physical chemistry. I dreaded leaving her and the children and looked forward to more of this upon my return.

As the RV door slammed, I started up the engine of the Ford F350. My mind switched gears into tournament mode, leaving all stress from the prior week's DUI and the Sam Sarazen reneging of his $1,000 debt in the rear-view mirror. I felt incredibly relieved knowing I was going to be taking a break from the pressure of my personal life, trading it into the pressure of tournament play for a few days.

I remember watching a Director's Cut of the first Jason Bourne movie, *Bourne Identity,* where the Director discussed that Jason, the lead character, while not even able to remember who he was or his training, was particularly calm and deadly during times of conflict. It was during the times of dealing with others and performing banal activities that got him stressed. There were some similarities in the way that Jason didn't know he was a highly trained assassin and I didn't know I was a highly trained *Buddha Golfer!*

I did my best not to speed as I made my way driving to Tamarisk to meet with "My Entourage" consisting of Dr. Tom and Gina *Magic* to get my mind and body primed correctly for the task ahead. Dr. Tom addressed my skeletal muscle immobility/pain and relaxed my contracted muscles. I felt the exhilaration in my circulatory system after each session, with my pain gone and my range of motion restored. My psyche was tuned by the Gina *Magic.* After both sessions, I quickly rolled a few putts on the super slick greens with my flex putter trainer just before hitting the road.

Somehow, I managed to pick-up Ward on time without any hiccups just outside the baggage claim. We stopped to fuel up before we hit the road. "Ward if you need to use the little boy's room or grab a beverage, well… giddy up!!" I continued circling my pointer finger in the air, "This is a non-stop flight, my Brother." Ward smiled in agreeance as he hustled through the door. The time was finally here… **Champions Tour School!**

We were off to an amazing start. Roughly two hours into our 3.5-hour drive to Goat Valley Country Club, the traffic on Hwy 15 came to a complete stop for an accident in the left lane. This wasn't really in my game plan today. I thought, d*on't freak out.* I attempted to visualize the bumper to bumper traffic as a *Buddha Field* with the cars transforming into multi-colored metallic lotus flowers, each lotus vehicle carrying Buddhas. I thought that the Buddha would have been proud of my improvisation.

As we began to move again, the car next to me abruptly changed lanes and cut me off. "Look out!" my brother Ward shouted. Normally the *bird* would fly, and explicit language would have immediately flown out of my mouth. Instead, I mentally blessed the driver *with greater awareness and consideration toward others on the road.* Each time I did this *mental blessing,* I noticed even greater serenity. As if by magic, my agitation stopped.

Normally my mood would worsen with each encounter, and my emotions would escalate, possibly with some tension in my neck or soreness in my throat.

Now, my negatives became positives. These **Techniques** were truly transformative, as each negative experience actually made me feel stronger and more mentally clear. Exercising these **Techniques** was a lot like weightlifting. Each time I worked out, I became stronger with more resistance (opposing force) and I felt happier and more confident. The remainder of the drive went smoothly without a hitch.

Whether the **Techniques** had a direct impact on my environment I couldn't say for sure. We did make record time and most assuredly my personal environment, meaning my mind, physiology, and emotions, were deeply impacted by the experience. Recently I read an article on how playing different music affected the taste of cheese. Hip Hop made it smellier, Zeppelin's *Stairway to Heaven* and Mozart's *Magic Flute* made it milder. I soon realized that if music could affect cheese, my *Buddha Nature* could probably affect a *Buddha Field.*

We soon arrived at our home for the next week. Upon arrival, my brother gave me an awkward look and didn't say a word. He had definitely noticed my abnormally calm demeanor.

After my 50th birthday back in August, I had packed up my RV and traveled on a small schedule of mini-tour events, and Monday qualifiers, to prepare for the **Champions Tour Regional Qualifying School.** I had played roughly 45 rounds of golf in the last 90 days, 28 of them in competition. I had rested most of the week leading up to it and felt prepared and confident going into the regional stage of qualifying.

I brought my brother, Ward, along with to caddie for me. He might not have the experience of Sam Sarazen, but he knew me. And, more importantly, I knew I wouldn't have to remind him of the 3 UPs to caddying... show UP, keep UP, and shut UP.

Ward was a scratch golfer and had a keen eye for reading the greens, and that would be a tremendous help. Especially with all that I had been through. I was happy to have him on the fairway with me along with the Buddhas in my *Buddha Field.*

As we arrived at the course, I could see people all over the parking lot arriving for practice rounds. I couldn't help but wonder if I might see Sam Sarazen this week since I knew he loved to caddie at *Tour School.* As each day I had become more Buddha-like, the drama over the unpaid bet and call from my boss Mr. Darman were waning. Since I hadn't reached full-blown enlightenment yet, there was still anger lingering within, and I hoped for Sam's sake, he wouldn't be here this week.

The practice rounds went well. Playing nine holes each of the two days conserved my energy. Only having to learn one course also made it easier. It was a beautiful course, and it gave me a chance to practice **Priceless Technique Number Three.**

After two days of 9-hole practice rounds, the time was finally here, and I was confident in my game plan leading into tomorrow's first round. I knew I wanted to limit my thoughts throughout each round, so I planned to have Ward keep score.

"Starting tomorrow, I will have you keep track of the scorecard for me, Ward, Ok?" I asked. "Sure," he replied.

This wasn't my first rodeo, and I wanted to focus my attention away from the score and more towards the *Points Game* that Gina *Magic* and I had co-created by eliminating thoughts of the score throughout the round. I focused more on commitment and staying disciplined.

I had been referred to her by several of my friends who said she had helped them become quite wealthy. She got the nickname "Magic" because they all had the same experience as if by *magic* people would call them for deals, or the deals would just appear out of nowhere. Her *magic* worked in my golf game too. What we visualized happened!

The *Points Game* consisted of: One point for hitting the Fairway, One for hitting the green, One for getting up and down regardless of the score, and One point for making a birdie or better. The goal was to score at least One point on every hole. This *Point Game* helps limit thoughts or worry about my score, position, quality of players in the field, and the number of spots advancing to the Finals. On top of that, I was excited to exercise my continued learning and usage of **The Three Priceless Techniques.**

"Let's head to the putting green and put in a little work before we call it a day." I said to Ward, "I love practicing with my new putting trainer- the Flex Putter." "Oh cool... Where did you get that?" Ward asked. "The Stockton's are promoting the product, and when I ran into Dave Jr., he gave me one to try." I continued, "Seriously, it has really helped me smooth out my putting stroke."

Earlier in the day a visual of the Buddha referencing **The Three Priceless Techniques** excitingly reminded me of *Three Simple Rules to Great Putting.*

"Do you know the *Three Simple Rules to Great Putting*, Ward?" I continued without waiting for his answer. "These *Three Simple Rules* saved my putting," I said. "Once I learned and adapted, my attitude regarding putting changed forever." Ward eagerly listening and grinning said, "Keep talking my brother, I'm all ears."

"OK, *Rule #1 Can you hit your spot?"* I stuck a tee perpendicular in the ground, starting from around one-foot rolling balls into the slender tee, moving back in 1-foot increments, as I went to work hitting my spot. Ward watched on as he asked, "How far back do you usually go?" "No more than a couple of feet from the cup at the most," I explained, "Whatever the shortest distance you can never miss. I hit about 18 putts, with an emphasis, getting the ball out of the hole after each putt."

"Let's move on to *Rule #2 "Can you control your speed?"* Starting from 20 feet and working my way up to 60 feet I took the same three balls and began rolling each ball across the length of the massive green. My aim was to stop the ball as close to the fringe as possible, without going off the putting surface. I did this about 18 times.

"And finally *Rule #3 "Can you read greens?"* "This is a learned art and does take time and practice. I commonly use a digital green reading level to document the slope on the playing surfaces." I continued telling Ward, "If you don't have one, you can purchase an App on your smartphone." Ward already knew this little PGA Tour secret, since we had charted and documented every green on property. We even documented visible drainage areas to get a feel for water drainage.

"Hey, thank you for showing me *the Three Simple Rules to Great Putting,* you've kept it a closely guarded secret for too long," Ward exclaimed. "You're welcome Ward," I said, "Once you become proficient at these *Three Simple Rules,* your putting will then be free of technical or mechanical thinking, and it will be about mental imagery." I was finally ready to share the *Three Simple Rules* with him; however, I wasn't yet ready to share the **Three Priceless Techniques**. *One step at a time,* I thought. *Much the same way the Buddha, as any great coach should sense, Ward wasn't quite ready yet for Parfection.*

"Mental imagery?" Ward said, with a puzzled look on his face. "Let me be more specific and give you a couple of examples," I said as I continued. "Jack Sherpa made it a habit to visualize the ball going into the hole at least three times before he would attempt to play that next shot." "Tiger, very similar to Jack, was taught by his father Earl to visualize the putt going into the hole. He and Earl referred to this as, "Putt to the Picture." "Any questions?" Ward was smiling, and I could see the light bulb had just come on as he responded, "No sir, that was awesome." He paused, then said, "I don't know about you, but I'm starving. Let's get some dinner." I nodded back. "I couldn't agree more." We were happy to call it a day.

On the next day, we drew the early tee time and got off to a hot start taking advantage of the perfect California weather with a -3 under par round of 69. I had been driving the ball quite well and put slightly better than average. My evening Flex Putter session had paid off. We spent the next few hours after lunch working to make sure I was still hitting my spot, and I continued to have the speed of the greens down pat. That would be the biggest factor to success on the extremely tricky putting surfaces at Goat Valley.

I hadn't really been challenged all day, and with few distractions, I was able to stay in my bubble and remain focused on the positives and stuck with my course game plan.

After returning to the RV, congratulatory messages began to roll in on social media and text messages from friends and family. As the afternoon turned to even, my mind began to wander with thoughts of my golfing future. From glory to past failures, I had a reel-to-reel playing in my head. I walked outside my RV into the parking area. I brought down the Buddha from heaven into my heart and expanded what I was now calling my *Buddha Suit.* I imagined rainbow light beaming out my heart in all ten directions. As I did this, all thoughts seemed to fade away. Next, in the progression, I imagined the area as a *Buddha Field* of luminous, golden light. Neither the past nor the future existed. In that very moment, I planted seeds within my consciousness for later exploration.

As I went back into my RV, I felt powerful, and I knew what had to be done. With a smile, I turned off my cell phone and tossed it into the drawer in the kitchen. With great surprise Ward blurted out, "That's right, we don't need, no stinking phones." I chuckled, "Thanks, Brother." *So far so good,* I thought, *this was easy!*

Round Four- Finding My *Buddha Fairway*

Things had gone extremely well for the first three days of the **Four Round Regional Qualifying School**. With rounds of 69, 71, 69, (-7) I had positioned myself inside the top 10 with 22 players advancing of 88 players in the field and a current cut line at -2 under par.

We had found a spot on the range. We began our pre-final round warm up like always, with a Driver teed up in slow motion as my first club. 10%, 20%, 30% and so on, until reaching 100% of full speed. This progression allowed proper body motion and built up speed control. I started warming-up this way in '05 after it had rained the night before. The range on a pretty steep uphill incline makes it super easy to chunky wedges, so I started teeing up the driver this way, and it stuck with me. Consequently, this made me a very exceptional driver of the ball.

We drew the 9:50 AM tee time, off the #1 tee, which meant we were in a good position to advance to the finals versus going off the #10 tee, which meant you were outside of the top 40 and very improbable to advance, though not impossible.

While my warmup went pretty well, I couldn't help but feel a bit uptight as we began to walk towards the practice putting green near the 1st tee, I looked over to see the giant Rolex clock next to the practice green. It was 9:37 AM, *just enough time to hit the locker room before tee time*, I believed.

As I walked into the locker room, I felt like my *Buddha Suit* was totally wrinkled and looked like I had slept in it. *"Old Andrew"* talk was beginning to rear his ugly head. His effort to pull my attitude into the dumps and create body tension spoke to how important this day was in my fantasy world. The pendulum from confidence to fear was swinging in the wrong direction. In order to stop it, I began to imagine the visions and voices moving farther away, making them impossible to see or hear…. Then they finally started to disappear.

I remembered during a mental training session with Gina *Magic;* she had talked about the Buddhist version of Angels. They were called *Dakinis*. Suddenly all the negatives disappeared from my consciousness, and it felt like my *Dakinis* had a warm iron that was smoothing the wrinkles out my *Buddha Suit.* The same change occurred when I brought the Golden Buddha down from heaven and into my heart. **Priceless Technique Number One** was the perfect antidote to my agitated state.

I made my way towards the 1st tee with the same semi-aggressive mindset as I had during the first three rounds. The plan was simple, get into the *Points Game,* manage my rhythm and tempo, and utilize **The Three Priceless Techniques** (or ***3PTs)*** during my four hours walk. I set my expectations high and was confident of greats results.

Upon arrival at the tee, I realized my pairing was with Charlie "The Cheater" Yama, who I had altercations within a previous tournament that year. He was known for his inability to score properly, for poor etiquette, and for making untimely noises during other player's shots. I remember him ripping the Velcro on his glove during several occasions during play the last time. His presence and nefarious tactics were definitely going to challenge me to stay focused on my game today. The **3PTs** would be critical!

When we shook hands on the tee, I noticed Charlie didn't have his clubs with him. "Where are your players' clubs?" asked the starter. "My caddie has them, don't you worry yourself old man they will be here," stated Charlie. I couldn't believe my eyes as I turned around to the noise of irons clanking against each other and of the staff bag hitting the ground… "Have you met Sam Sarazen?" Charlie asked with a huge grin on his mug. With his sarcastic tone and facial expression, he clearly knew all about my past with Sam.

"Oh, we've have met," I stated, with blatant disregard in an attempt to prevent the pendulum from swinging back. I imagined that Sam heard it as "We've met bitch." Without even looking in their direction, I stared down the fairway with my nervous system in a panic. My heart starting to race, and my grip got a bit tight and shaky. I tried desperately to make the 1st fairway become a *Buddha Fairway.* I remembered my first TV, back in the day when remote controls didn't exist, when we had to use *rabbit ears* instead of a cable to hone in on the best reception. Like those old rabbit ears, I was trying to adjust my consciousness into a *Buddha Field (Fairway),* because now it felt more like a battlefield.

While trying to apply **Priceless Technique Number Two,** I realized that it was the misapplication of **Priceless Technique Number Three** that was blowing up my Buddha world. *I am not going to shake hands with that asshole,* I thought to myself. "Take a deep breath," Ward whispered into my ear. "Don't let him get to you." Ward knew the past between Sam, and I ended poorly.

"How's the swing coming along?" Sam asked, knowing damn well I hated that. I turned towards Sam and gave him the thumbs up. "Thank you for asking," I replied as I put my glove on and prepared to hit my first tee shot of the event. Sam continued, "*Double A* has *rabbit ears*, so we're going to have to be quiet Charlie." "Is that right?" Charlie said as they both gurgled under their breath. *Fuck...* I thought. *this guy is literally in my head...* I had just been thinking of *rabbit ears* and then Sam using this phrase. *How did he know that? Holy Fuck!* I deliberated. My *Buddha Suit* was now in tatters, and it was only the first freakin' hole.

I reflected to my high school biology class where I learned the word deuterostome. Due to the unique and hysterical definition, I had always remembered it. Humans are deuterostomes meaning that in the womb they develop the anus before any other opening. Which basically meant at one point in a person's life they were nothing more than an asshole. It appeared Sam never developed past this stage, as he was truly a deuterostome.

The first few holes didn't quite go as we had planned. I drove into the rough on one, which resulted in a birdie putt, only to have another long birdie putt on three, as well. I was so nervous and attached that I even forgot that *the Three Simple Rules to Great Putting* would stop me from a three-putt on the 3rd hole. On top of that, I had completely forgotten my *Points Game. I needed no more three putts and much more* ***3PTs,*** I insisted.

On the 4th hole, I missed a short 7-foot birdie chance when a PGA Tour rules official pulled up on our group and accidentally slammed on the breaks, which distracted me during my stroke causing another disastrous 3 putt. Standing on the side of the green I stared at the official throwing imaginary daggers his direction as if he had purposefully slammed on the breaks. The Buddha showed what others' negative energy did me. Sadly, I was now understanding at a deeper level that I was doing the same thing. I felt powerless to stop it. 3 putts replaced **3PTs**.

Two holes later, on the 6th green, I was standing over a 22-foot putt for birdie. Charlie and Sam began whispering, again, knowing damn well I had *rabbit ears.* I should have stepped out of that shot. Instead, I went ahead and hit the putt *anyways,* sending the ball sailing 6 feet beyond the cup. At that moment, I couldn't help but laugh at myself. I walked up to mark my ball, and said, "I'll wait." As I quickly slid a dime behind my ball.

I was laughing because it was Sam Sarazen who had named these uncharacteristic shots, an *anyways*.

Basically, any shot that I wasn't 100% committed to and went ahead and hit it was considered an *anyways.* Sam wouldn't hesitate to call me out saying, "You weren't fully committed and detached from the outcome, yet, you hit it *anyways.*"

How could I let them get to me? I asked myself. As my hands shook in anger, I stood behind my marker looking over the 6-foot comebacker. *Focus man, breath, you can do this.* I tried to bring down the Buddha, and once I couldn't feel it, the other techniques were pointless even to try. More self-talk ensued as my mind wandered with *Old Andrew* manning the helm of my sinking ship. I hadn't visualized the putt going in as I stood there attempting to gather myself. I walked up to the putt, but my mind was all over the place. I drew the putter blade back quicker than normal and missed my spot. I had pulled the par putt fractions to the left. My hopes of *parfections* turned to par fractions… "Fuck, another bogey!" I yelled out.

This aftershock of a shaky beginning to the final round was starting to create massive stress, and I could feel my anxiety escalating. "I wish I could make Sam disappear, just like the last three days when I didn't know he was around," I said to Ward. I somehow was able to make pars on the next three holes as I made the turn, a front nine score of +2, 38.

On the 10th green I had a pretty slick downhill putt and ran the putt 5' past the hole, "I'll mark," I told my playing partners. I began walking around the hole stalking the putt like a madman, even though I had just seen the ball go by the hole and saw the break. As I stepped over the putt, I couldn't help having *rabbit ears* again even though nobody was speaking. I could hear everything around me, as I pulled the putter back completely unfocused with zero rhythm… the ball didn't even touch the hole, as I had pulled hooked another putt a good 1/2 inch to the left. I was doing what had failed me in the past, trying to make things perfect.

Now beginning to panic, as we waited on the 11th tee I stared down the fairway at arguably the toughest hole on the course, a 495-yard par 4 that was back into the fan. Just the sight of Sam made me nauseous as we waited for the group in front of us to clear the fairway.

Standing there, I thought to myself, *Seeing Arya and the children as Buddhas and seeing the other drivers as Buddhas, was easy. But how could I possibly see myself as a Buddha while I golf?* I was starting to feel my *Buddha Suit* thought it was only partially clinging to my body now. It felt like I was dragging the remnants along with the rough patches of grass.

With each shot, it seemed like I had never played golf before, let alone professionally for 30 years. As we approached the 18th green I had just hit my final full shot with an 8 iron to 20 feet. I was taking deep breaths, working very hard to re-apply my Buddha splendor. I managed to scrape it around with my B game and had this sense that I may need to make this 20-foot putt to advance to the Finals. I could feel *"Old Andrew" talk* starting in, my *Buddha Suit* was sparking as if it was about to ignite into flames. I had heard of spontaneous combustion, and I now believed it was possible.

As I approached the putt, I could feel the negatives in full force and *Old Andrew* playing memories of every putt I had ever missed, in my head. I did my best to breathe through the putt, *don't be afraid to make the putt,* I said to myself. I nervously limped the ball up to the hole, and the *Old Andrew* mind flooded with *thoughts of technique,* as had been the case most of the day.

Somehow the ball ended 1' from the cup, and I was able to tap in for a par for a rather ugly round of (+3) 75 and a 4-day total of (-4) 284 strokes. Hopefully, this would be good enough to advance to the Finals that December 1-4.

I wasn't convinced we had sealed the deal as we waited for all the groups to finish; It was becoming more and more apparent this was going be a close call. Even with the event completed, I still struggled to feel empowered and *Buddha-like.* I had lost my game during the round and was disappointed with my overall mental stability under the pressures of tour golf. *Was Sam Sarazen becoming my Kryptonite?*

I had dipped lower than my lowest *Old Andrew* and truly knew my application of **The Three Priceless Techniques** during the round today was nonexistent. I had moved so far forward, at least so I thought. That day, I had regressed backward even further. My breathing had become labored, and the tension in my shoulders was tighter than ever. I had anxiety like I hadn't felt in a long time--almost Xanax territory. *What a loser,* I said to myself.

I thought if I did a body scan and were observant, my body would tell me what I needed to do. Awareness is a powerful thing.

Before the initial Buddha dream, I was more somber than depressed. I had felt bliss and peace and had a pretty good professional career record. After I woke up discovered what feeling depressed was like, and it hit me like a brick. More than anything I wanted to have inner peace. This inability to control my mental game and my emotions were unprecedented.

I looked around the room only to spot Sam sitting across the room watching me. The smile on his face let me know he was enjoying my anguish. My heart pounded with rage with what I was seeing, and my hands began to sweat uncontrollably. My thoughts sped up like the final lap of a stock car race in my dome. I replayed the Buddha repeatedly in my head but couldn't get a grip on my mental and physical power over this particular situation.

The **Three Priceless Techniques** were truly priceless and now appeared as if they were no longer afforded to me. My inner dialogue went to a negative place. My *Old Andrew talk* was destroying my *Buddha outfit.* I was starting to doubt that I could succeed in applying these **Techniques**. *Sure, these Techniques worked in dreams, but this was real life, after all,* I pondered.

As I stared at the scoreboard counting the same names over and over as scores came in, I wondered about trying for my fate. My brother could tell I was not in a great place considering somehow; I ended up in a tie with Charlie "The Cheater" Yama. Ward was aware of my unsuccessful **2005 PGA Tour School** personal tie for 21st by myself to miss by one shot, and how that had affected me long term.

Like any great sibling, Ward began reassuring me, "You're going to make it Andrew." I loved his confidence, but I wasn't convinced yet. I said, "Ward, look at Sam Sarazen staring at us, with that devilish grin like he just stole your wallet and you can't prove it." Ward turned with a squint in his eye that I hadn't seen before as if to question me, "Charlie Yama is tied with you." He continued, "If Charlie doesn't make it, Sam doesn't make it either." I thought about what Ward had just said, and I felt like a complete idiot.

I did my best to reconfigure while taking deep breaths and visualizing myself at the **Champions Tour Finals** in two weeks. I was determined to separate myself from this *Old Andrew* funk, by applying **The Three Priceless Techniques**. After a few minutes, I still wasn't feeling very Buddha-like, concluding I had reached 34% at best. I just couldn't let go of Sam Sarazen laughing at me, and even though my brother was probably right, the hatred lingered.

While retrieving myself from the depths of anguish and disappointment, I worked on returning to a semi-Buddha perspective. I reflected upon the gamut of emotions of the day's round resolving that I wanted to maintain this tranquil abiding state of being that the Buddha referenced in the dream. It was at that moment, I made a mental resolution to end my emotional dismay. I looked over at Sam Sarazen and smiled in an effort to calm my mind. Earlier I remembered wishing I could make him disappear, then EUREKA it hit me! While *physically* I couldn't make him disappear, I could make him *psychically* disappear, meaning his imposition on my psyche.

For the first time all day I felt a jolt of confidence. Some semblance of hope was bubbling up from somewhere deep inside. Pivoting from its nadir the pendulum was moving, and it was moving in the right direction. I attempted to see Sam as a Buddha dressed in a *Saffron Buddha Suit.* Feeling inspired and hoping for any glimmer of hope, I kind of fudged the technique a little and disregarded the *Buddha Suit* and just tried to see him as *blinding light.* I always liked the U2 song *City of Blinding Lights.* It often gave me goosebumps. I think I may have even hummed the song while applying the **3PTs.** I didn't think the Buddha would mind...

IT WORKED!!! Sam had begun disappearing. He was turning into light. In fact, everything was turning into light. The fairway was transforming into light, into a *Buddha Fairway.* Charlie, Ward, and especially I, were transforming into light. I think I heard the word *Rigpa* in my mind. I chuckled for a moment when I thought of the word Fairway sounded eerily like *Fairy-way*, but I didn't care, I didn't think the Buddha would mind either, as I was laughing for the first time all day. *That was his whole point, right? To see past the illusion.* I didn't know what Rigpa was, but the fairies were probably like *Dakinis*, and they were starting to work with me, here. The darkness of my world was transforming into light!

Less than five minutes had passed before the lead PGA Tour official emerged to post the results and list of advancing players and alternates. I held my breath as Ward, and I approach the list only to see with great relief I had finished and tied for the 20th position. I was advancing to the finals! I turned to Ward, "Boo-yah" as he wrapped his arms around me, we jumped up and down in elation. "I'm so proud of you Brother, you did it." Grinning ear to ear and almost in tears I responded, "Thank you for being a part of it, I love you, man!"

Enhanced with a letter from the **Champions Tour** and advancing me to the finals, I still wasn't feeling anything close to 100% *Buddha-like,* but I was better. About 20 minutes into the drive home I recalled a conversation with the Buddha conveying that, "To become *Buddha-like* it would take practice, commitment, mistakes and time." I remembered telling the Buddha, "Golf is exactly the same way; it requires *practice, commitment, mistakes, and discipline*." I was hoping it wouldn't take long for me to act Buddha-like regularly. "34% was certainly better than 100% of being *Old Andrew* like." The awareness of my self-talk was really coming to the forefront of my consciousness.

And, more importantly, I was able to distinguish which voice was winning*; Old Andrew or Buddha-like Andrew.*

The 3 ½ hour drive went smoothly, and dinner tasted even better. However, I still wasn't convinced I had this Buddha mind conquered. The $1,000 Sam still owed me was on the front of my lobe. During the drive home, I again, visualized the cars and truck on the freeway as metallic lotus flowers hovering above the road carrying their Buddhas home safely. This visualization made me laugh inside, and I was confident that the Buddha would like my improvisation of **Techniques Two and Three**. I was much more relaxed and smiling more often with the upcoming opportunity of **Champions Tour School Finals** in my future. I made it home 12 minutes faster than my phone app Waze had calculated and without speeding.

The Family greeted me with open arms and congratulatory cheers. The younger ones were just loving on me because I was home, unaware that Daddy had accomplished the first half of a very long-term goal. The connection amongst us was unbelievably close, and we were becoming more in-tune; as my energy field expanded the energy field of those around me expanded too. The confidence that everyone had in me had created a collective field of energy, and we all melted into one. Our golden and rainbow energy merged into one large, powerful field. The Buddha briefly mentioned that he'd speak with me again about the power of groups, and I was looking forward to that conversation.

The new ability to sense this energetic connection with others became precious to me. I reflected upon my poor interactions as with one of our dogs, got out of control like a wildfire of verbal lashings, and over only a golf travel bag. I had raised my voice so loudly that the entire house was on edge. But all of that no longer mattered and I was enamored with how everyone was glowing so brightly with positivity. My love for them was extra magnified. It was absolutely incredible how we had made our home into a *Buddha Field* with so many powerful Buddhas radiating rainbow lights coaxial to infinity.

Once my head hit my pillow, as I sank into the cold sheets of desert winter, I began to review my week. Overall, I was quite pleased that I had advanced to the Finals. I was pleased with myself for grinding out my final round when it could have easily been an 80. Everything was just as the Buddha had described it, with hurdles to jump and bumps to avoid. Overall, I had been winning at elevating my consciousness, and willingly shared the Buddha energies with everyone around. Of course, there would always be down moments to overcome; however, I was extremely confident I would end on top. I had never had the glass ¾ full feeling before in my life, and I felt like it was there to stay. My mind and body felt very light, seemingly able to sense my Theta brain softly slipping into a deep dormancy.

As I slept, my consciousness was taken to a *Buddha Field*. Back on the *Buddha Balcony,* the Buddha praised me for my accomplishments and the ability to keep it together even when things didn't look good. The Buddha's presence was incredibly powerful, and I seemed even more receptive to his knowledge. *Wide awake,* I wondered, *is that even possible in a dream?* I amused myself. *How can I get better at* ***Priceless Technique Number Three*** *while I play the game of golf?*

I chortled again at myself as I thought, "What had I just muttered under my breath?" Do Buddhas even play golf? Neither the Buddha's demeanor nor facial expressions changed in the slightest way although it seemed the Buddha was amused by my thoughts.

The Buddha, with a serious and direct tone in his voice, said, "Andrew, allowing yourself to climb aboard what would be synonymous to an amusement park ride is *un-Buddha like*. Remember earlier how easy it was to see yourself as a Buddha, versus a golfer?" This is a human tendency that you must endeavor to transcend. The ups and downs, and the highs and lows on an emotional ride are only based on the perception of the physical world–a transitory world--a golfer's world," he said.

"Golf is a game of inches. The most important is the six inches between your ears," the Buddha said. Before he continued, he could see my exuberance and allowed me to interject. "That's a famous Arnold Palmer quote. Did you teach the **Three Priceless Techniques** to Arnold Palmer???" were the words that burst out of my mouth.

The Buddha basically ignored my question and continued with "Always remember Andrew, the *tranquil abiding* part of the teachings. You must maintain a sense of peace and tranquility always, no matter what is happening around you."

"Past your physical body, you have an energy body called your Inner Aura. Past that are bodies that are more energetically refined. Your Emotional aka Astral Body contains the sum of your emotions. Think of it as your emotional blueprint. It can hold every emotion from the lowest of depression, shame, and guilt to the higher end with peace, euphoria, and ecstasy. Your Mental Body carries all your thoughts, beliefs, observations, and viewpoints."

"Many golfers try to play in a *No Mind, Zen State, or Flow State.* It is nearly impossible to do when your Emotional Body is agitated. Think of trying to see the bottom of a lake when the surface of the water is turbulent; it is impossible. With meditation and the application of the **Techniques,** you can calm your Emotional Body."

"At the same time, the Mental Body is filled with thoughtforms or what the Buddhists call *Chitta*--most people's Mental Bodies are filled with *shitta."* After this long and thorough explanation, he finished it off with humor. I smiled, as the Buddha always shocked me with an occasional joke. I believed he used wit to help me remember seemingly foreign concepts. For, a microsecond, I saw myself off into the future sharing these **Techniques** with others. His brilliant teaching style was to help prepare me for the future.

"Zen Buddhism came from Japan," the Buddha explained. It was a renaming of Chan Buddhism which hailed from China. The origin of both methods came out of India and was known as *Dhyan.* Meditation and application of the **3PTs** will polish the Mental Body. We'll talk more about meditation in the future."

"For now, I'm going to teach you a simple breathing exercise called *Dhyan Breathing.* In the orient powerful secrets tend to be hidden from the masses and watered down. Many people have great challenges emptying their mind and emotions without meditation and this breath. Using your willpower to clean the slate of your mind is difficult to work and times a long time to achieve favorable results. It is far easier to apply this breath," he sagaciously said. I mimicked the Buddha doing the *Dhyan Breath.* Whoa! He was right! Now that he pointed out these bodies, I could feel them. My Emotional and Mental became still with my inner tempo slowing, and my *Zen State* greatly increased. This was far easier than any of the techniques I had previously learned.

The Buddha continued, "There are three main types of Buddhism. Hinayana (The Lesser Vehicle), Mahayana (the Great Vehicle), and Vajrayana (The Thunderbolt or Diamond Vehicle). The Buddha in 500 B.C. prophesized that the next Buddha, Padmasambhava, which means "Born of the Lotus," would bring Buddhism to the land of the Snows. This prophecy was fulfilled with Padmasambhava bringing Buddhism to Tibet in the 8th Century."

The Buddha wisely paused. This was a lot of information to take in. This information was far beyond the game of golf—It was important to my game of life. As the Buddha could see I was comprehending what he said, "Hinayana and Mahayana are the Sutra path. What I'm teaching you is from the Tibetan Vajrayana path, which is the Tantric path of achieving enlightenment. This can be achieved through connecting to your true self, your *Buddha self, t*hus you are learning *Tantric Golf."*

My voice went up two octaves, and my body moved excitedly as I impulsively asked, "Buddha, what does golf have to do with sex???" I wisecracked. "Nothing," he said, "unless you are doing them both right, and then you will be in a state of "No Mind." "This Divine State of *No Mind* is why you say, "Oh My God" after great sex and after a great shot."

I again nearly fell off the *Buddha Balcony* with laughter. I knew he was making a joke, so I could pass it along when I shared it with others in the future. I pondered what he said. *He was right. I realized why I and others played golf and liked sex so much. These were one of the few times there was NO thought and there was ecstasy.* Everything was starting to make sense now on so many levels. I was getting it!

The Buddha continued, "Your unconscious mind makes 99.3% of all decisions. When you are in the *Flow State* you are not accessing the unconscious mind. However, when the unconscious mind is being directed by your *Buddha Nature,* you are embodying the ultimate *Flow State*, which is beyond space and time." *This sounded much like the words of "Mr. 59" Al Geiberger from a 1977 quote he made after shooting the lowest score in the history of the PGA Tour,* I pondered.

"I've come to realize that I perform best when I'm letting my subconscious mind hit the ball and my conscious mind is otherwise occupied," I revealed. I began to see too many coincidences here and suspected the Buddha had worked with some of the greats *but had he taught Mr. 59 as well?* I believed I was beginning to make headway on these Buddha concepts at a much deeper level.

"My Beloved Andrew, let me help you with a few more methods to perfect **Priceless Technique Number Three.** These methods will aid you in dealing with other distractions like people moving in the gallery, noise in the background, or when playing with unpleasant people," the Buddha declared.

"The normal **Technique** is to visualize the person in the form of a Buddha, as you have done." "You intuited the more advanced **Technique** when you played the U2 song in your head and turned everything and everyone into blinding lights. By dissolving their physical bodies, into formless white light, like a ball of energy with consciousness--it helps you detach from your perception of their human qualities." "Well done," he clarified with a hint of praise.

The Buddha took a beat and paused, allowing time for this concept to sink in. Observing when it had, he proceeded. "This **Technique** will be easier to use on others, who don't have your best interest in mind, because you can depersonalize your *Samsaric*, physical world. **Priceless Technique Number Three** is changing your perception of people so that you realize we are all one gigantic energy field. Physically, yes, we are individuals, however spiritually we are all one," he so beautiful proclaimed.

The Buddha's deep insight comforted me.

"I would like to add another method that will help you get to **Priceless Technique Number Three** with greater regularity," the Buddha went on. "Try to visualize any person as your own mother, this will help you develop compassion for others," the Buddha explained.

My own mother!? I mentally interjected. *Trying to visualize Sam Sarazen as my mother was going to be difficult, but I would try,* I thought to myself.

At that very moment, I realized that in this dream state with the Buddha, thinking thoughts and speaking were the same. In all previous dreams, we had communicated through a kind of telepathy, without our lips moving. I made a mental note to later ask the Buddha more regarding our special communicating abilities.

"Yes, your mother," the Buddha responded. Reading my mind, the Buddha further explained, "Your mother experienced great pain delivering you. She fed you. She changed your diapers and kept you safe. She also made many sacrifices for your betterment. A mother loves her child more than she loves herself. If you visualize every human as your mother and treat them with the same level of love, compassion, and respect, in time it will help you overcome your negative tendencies. You can limit your negative projections towards others, which have been breaking your concentration causing you to pass the blame onto others for your shortcomings.

After a long pause, the Buddha went on to say, “When exposed to people like Sam or to little movements and noises during your practice or driving range time, you won’t be as distracted. Wouldn’t you agree?” The Buddha continued, “However, during tournament golf, you seem to elevate the importance of a particular round and or a specific tournament.” The Buddha continued by saying, “This illusion that one round of golf has greater importance over another creates suffering via three of the *Five Poisons;* attachment, delusion, and hatred.”

I’m learning a lot here, but there is still so much education ahead, I speculated.

“I will give you another method, Andrew, since you will be sharing these **Three Priceless Techniques** with others. You will need different strategies for different people. For people with *pride* and *ego* as their stumbling block, they can rapidly diminish this *pride* by visualizing others as a Buddha and prostrating at their feet,” the Buddha elucidated.

"Prostrate?" ejaculated out of my mouth. I thought *you have got to be kidding me*… I exclaimed, "How can you prostrate in front of someone you don't really respect?" "I mean seriously, first you want me to visualize Sam as my mother, and now you expect me to prostrate to Sam?" I stared at the Buddha in disbelief.

The Buddha responded patiently, "Wouldn't you prefer working off the karma of the relationship this way--by mentally doing prostrations to overcome your own pride? Or, would you rather maybe, lose your own prostate?" *Was the Buddha making a dirty joke to emphasize the correlation or was this just my imagination?* I was beginning to understand the Buddha at a much higher level and felt as if maybe some of my bad habits and humor were being cleared.

In another Planck moment, I heard *Skillful Means* in my head like the Buddha had telepathically put it there.

The Buddha paused allowing me time to reflect. When he continued, he said, "When pride is a major hurdle, life will trip you up. Pride can cause financial problems, relationship challenges, and health issues. Pride will drop you to your knees. It is up to you how you decide to shrink your ego. You can do physical prostrations or mental prostrations to negate this pride, or you can have painful real-life scenarios that will get your attention and drive you to the floor. The choice is up to you, Andrew."

Inside I sniggered, *looks like in either of the above cases I was going to be on the floor. At least with doing a prostration, it was like combining a pushup with a burpee, and I'd get buff. I was going to make this illusion a good one and look Buddha hot!*

Once the Buddha had mentioned being shackled by chains, and this was the second time the Buddha had been so lovingly direct with me. I when presented this way, the Buddha's teaching along with his demeanor, had a fatherly aspect to it. It moved me. It nudged me out of my own ego and into the realization that this technique may work. And...I really needed to make it work. I realized that I still had some pride to work on. Imagining myself prostrating to a person full of pride would be challenging to my ego at first, but I believed that it would be very, very effective.

I had been extremely thrown off by my final round pairing with Charlie "The Cheater" Yama and Sam earlier in the day, so I took control of the dream. The *Buddha Balcony* was a great laboratory for testing theories. *I realized the Balcony was there for my sole betterment.* I laughed, *the word sole in sole betterment was assuredly soul betterment. I loved the realizations I had been making from time to time with the Buddha.*

I continued testing the prostration concept. *Since we are all one, if others have pride, I must have pride as well.* I could feel my *Buddha Suit* looking pretty dapper. I started at first with a bow, common practice in Tokyo, Japan. I felt the area around my heart, and the top of my head expand. *So far so good,* I said to myself.

Maybe it was my pride, but I felt like I had to transform Sam Sarazen into a bigger Buddha to prostrate in his general direction. I had viewed Sam Sarazen as evil and perceived his smaller issues as his ego. My *Buddha Suit* now felt like it needed a trip to the cleaners as I was clearly judging Sam. In my mind, I worked hard to completely transform Sam into a huge Golden Buddha. I initiated the prostrating at Sam's now Buddha's feet.

After about the third mental prostration, it was as if the dry cleaner's soap was washing my *Buddha Suit* and I started to feel like I had become an even bigger Golden Buddha. *Hmmm...* I considered, *maybe whatever I see myself prostrating to, I become? Color me Buddha Mind blown!*

I wasn't sure if I could prostrate to Sam anymore. The Buddha watched as I contemplated what to do next. The Buddha turned towards me and like nothing he had done previously began prostrating in my direction. His face transformed into the likeness of Sam Sarazen directly in front of me. His eyes softened, and he actually smiled. He said, "Andrew, a diamond has many facets, the truth has many levels, Illusions have many purposes. When I prostrated to him in return, the Buddha's face faded back to itself and very calmly he began talking. "It is good that you are helping Sam reach his potential as a Buddha. As you develop further, we'll work on **Techniques** for someone who has evil intent and how to minimize it." I nodded in acknowledgment.

"Lastly, Andrew, there is a simple Technique that can be done anywhere anytime. It is particularly great in a business situation, where you do not have a lot of time, and you find yourself losing your cool. You can mentally visualize the other person as a Buddha and say *Namaste*. Namaste simply means, the Buddha within me salutes the Buddha within you. This method will help melt away the mental, emotional and karmic obscurations that you have for the other person, and that they have for you. The more challenged the relationship is, the more you need to do **Namaste Technique**. Your connections with others travel at different levels, but let's save that for another time." Excited for a chance to test these **Techniques,** I turned to the Buddha with a huge grin and shouted out "Namaste!" The Buddha started laughing for just a second, showing me a side of him I hadn't seen before. I felt his joyful energy running through my veins like a nicotine rush after your first hit off a cig. As the Buddha disappeared into the depths of my dream, "I floated back into my suspended sleeping consciousness."

The Finals

I'd been chomping at the bit for the last two weeks, and it was finally time to play. It worked out perfectly that this year the final stage of **Champions Tour School** was about 50 miles from my home, making it easy to get in a few practice rounds. It felt like I was the home team in the NFL with an automatic 3-point bookmaker advantage in Las Vegas. I played the golf course a few times in the weeks preceding the event and felt pretty good about my knowledge of the layout. I knew I really needed to take this course seriously since I had yet to shoot in the '60s in any of my previous rounds on this course.

Earlier in the week, I had scheduled two practice rounds, one for early morning and the other around noon, I wanted to duplicate my playing times and gain a better feel for all day playing conditions, especially if the wind kicked up.

After finishing our second practice round, I said to Ward, "I will get our tee times and meet you at the RV." I cut through the massive clubhouse searching for the location of the first and second round tee times. As I worked my way through the maze-like clubhouse, I made my way to the already locked golf shop door. The shop being closed was understandable since we had pretty much played until dark. As I scanned the list for my day for my tee time, it was listed as 8:20 AM with yep-- you guessed it--Charlie “The Cheater” Yama for the first two rounds. That meant Sam Sarazen would probably be there as well. This should not have been a shock to me since we had tied in the **Regional Qualifying School** just two weeks ago. Somehow, I knew to test my ability to the use of the **Three Priceless Techniques** was imminent.

After returning to the RV, Ward and I enjoyed a nice dinner of Carne Asada crockpot style that had been prepared that morning. I said to Ward, “Whoa, this Carne is amazing my brother.” “Thanks, Bro.” We each had a glass of wine as we reminisced about our childhood, laughing ourselves to sleep in the comfy quarters of the two bed RV. As the room became silent, I could hear Ward’s deep breathing as he quickly fell asleep. I closed my eyes and imagined myself on the 1st tee staring down my *Buddha Fairway* and I hit my first tee shot inside my head. I walked off the end of the tee towards the *Buddha Fairway* while I started my countdown, *Ten, nine, eight, seven, six, five, four, three…Zzzz*

I hadn’t used an alarm clock to wake up in the morning since my honorable discharge from the USAF in the mid-’90s. I woke up as per usual around 5:00 AM to stretch out my stiff 50--aging--old body and go through my usual morning routine. With one exception, I took an extra moment to prostrate towards Sam Sarazen and visualize him as a radiant golden Buddha, without judgment or name calling.

I imagined myself donned in my best *Buddha Suit* and my favorite Black Clover hat standing on the driving range with Charlie Yama and several other competitors. I began to visualize the entire golf course as a *Buddha Field,* with *Buddha Fairways* protected by lotus flowers. I further imagined these lotus flowers helping to magically guide my ball to the perfect landing spot each time. Every player had the appearance of golden orbs flowing together in the brightest of lights. I really felt ready for my day and knew the Buddha would be happy for me.

We arrived at the club at around 6:30 AM as I usually preferred to be awake at least 2-3 hours prior to teeing off, ensuring I was awake and ready to go. We headed to the restaurant for a quick bowl of oatmeal and fruit before making our way to the practice facilities. *"*Nothing better than a little brain food before golf,*"* I said to Ward. He was not a fan as I noted the disgusted look on his face. "Yuck."

Upon arrival at the clubs practice facility, we weren't shocked the first people we had run into were Charlie and Sam. I took a deep breath making no eye contact with either of them or anyone else as I walked the length of the range. Ward could sense my discomfort and said, "They are going to be here all week so you might as well settle in." Knowing Ward was correct I imagined myself in my *Buddha Super Hero Suit* with the cape magically hovering in the air, I quietly acknowledged.

The practice facilities at Q School were always busy with players. Each player in the finals had designated hitting spots stacked with a pyramid of ProV-1x Titleist golf balls. I can attest that hitting a ProV-1x on the range is pretty freakin' awesome!

Finding my designated stall, I dropped my alignment stick on the teeing ground and went to work going through the first half of my range routine. I teed up the Driver like always, swinging slow motion, hitting a few balls around 30 yards, then 50, 75, 100, working my way up to full speed and distance.

Once loose and ready to play, I removed the alignment stick from the ground and began working on target and ball awareness. "I am almost ready to go," I reassured Ward "I just want to make I'm hitting it where I was looking and clear my mind of technical thoughts." "You're the Boss," Ward replied. As I began to finish up, I glanced over at the giant clock on the putting green, 7:55 AM. I nodded to Ward, "Quick trip to the head and I will meet you at the practice putting green." I said. Ward nodded back.

We met at the green, and I started my warm-up putting session by hitting putts from 1, 2, and 3 feet from the cup, and retrieving the ball out of the hole after each made putt. I then grabbed my Flex-putter and began putting 40 footers back and forth across the green. To finish up I used an alignment stick, putting balls parallel along the stick to revalidate my eye line and ball position one last time before heading to the 10th tee.

Once on the tee, our starter passed out scorecards and we ended with Charlie Yama's card. Snickering to myself, as I thought of a potential incident happening today was highly probable.

"Keep an eye on Charlie today would you please?" I reminded Ward, "You got it." Ward replied.

To my surprise, Charlie Yama clearly showed up to play. He was playing extremely well, so well it was all we could do to keep up with his pace of play.

"This guy's actually quite good," Ward said.

Funny thing is I had just thought that myself, *why in the world would he cheat?* "He doesn't need to cheat," I said to Ward.

Ward knew I needed to focus on my game and cocoon into my concentration, so he kept a close eye on Charlie. After waiting all day to see anything odd, only to see nothing but great play, Ward commented. "Maybe it was just a bad rumor."

During the time I was watching Charlie tear it up, I had completely forgotten about Sam Sarazen. I had made him a Buddha this morning before arriving at the range, and it seemed to be working. I was having fun again, so much fun that we were already standing on # 18 tee. "It's unbelievable, I can't believe we're on #18," I said to Sam and Charlie as I continued, "I could probably go 36 holes." We all hooted as if it was just another round with my buddies from home.

Was this the subconscious mind that the Buddha referenced? I wondered.

Ward and I had stuck to our game plan while enjoying a walk through the lotus flowers of the *Buddha Fairway.* Charlie and I had both hit perfect drives center cut on #18 and hopefully only needed one more iron shot.

After factoring in elevation, temperature, and wind, Ward and I agreed the shot would be in play a little longer than normal and decided on a 175-yard 7 iron from 155 yards. Keeping the flight low, my ball pierced through the slight breeze that had picked up over the last couple finishing holes as we turned back towards the clubhouse. "Nice shot!" Ward said as he handed me the putter.

When we arrived at the extremely elevated green, I could see my ball 10 feet from the cup for a birdie. Circling the cup like a vulture over prey, my feet were firmly grounded to the green, and I was completely immersed in the energy of the *Buddha Field.*

There was no question I was going to make the putt, as I squatted behind the ball, and three times visualizing the ball rolling over the front of the cup. I stepped into the putt with intention, I could see the ball in the hole, and my *job* was to go get that ball out of the hole just like I had practiced on the green many times before teeing off. *Putt to the Picture* as Tiger's dad taught him. I whispered as I walked into the putt with my mind clear of technical thoughts. After a couple of deep breaths, I rolled the ball along the ground on what appeared to be a great line directly into the center of the pin. As it made that epic sound of the ball dropping to the bottom of the hole, I was elated. I attempted to damper my smile as I shook hands with Charlie and Sam as we exited the green and headed for the Scoring area.

As we sat down in the Score tent, both Charlie and Sam congratulated me on my play, "That was a fine round," Charlie exclaimed. "What did you shoot?" Sam asked. I really wasn't sure; I was having so much fun playing the *Points Game* and implementing the **3 PTs** that I lost track of my score just like we had hoped.

Standing behind my chair and looking over my shoulder at my card, my brother barked out, "66 six under par is what I have tied with you, Charlie." I smiled as I looked at Charlie, "great round yourself, looking forward to tomorrow." We signed our cards after triple checking the score and then headed for the range to warm down for an hour before a nap and a well-deserved steak dinner.

The Final Round

The second and third rounds went pretty much without a hiccup with rounds of 66, 69, 69 and a 1 shot lead at -12 under par with 18 holes to play. With only eigth players advancing with fully exempt status, the heated pressure to play well was on everyone to perform their best.

I had put **The Three Priceless techniques** to the test and felt like I was progressing well; however, we still had the final round to play, and that would be the true test.

That morning I felt like I was at the spiritual gym getting ready to hit the heavy weights section. The heavier weights with greater resistance, build bigger muscles, or in this case, more developed spiritual muscles.

As we arrived at the course for breakfast like each day prior, I began to rework myself into a Buddha entering a Buddha Field mentally. I visualized everyone on the driving range and practice putting green as a Buddha emitting gold and then rainbow light, especially Sam Sarazen. I had made a major transformation in the way I saw Sam, and I was now actually grateful for him in some odd way. Rather than seeing him as the guy I had fired for his mouth or the guy that owed me $1,000. I saw him as a vehicle for my own personal growth and as a teacher.

I concentrated on him being the brightest and lightest Buddha on the range. I had visualized the entire golf course as a gigantic *Buddha Field* with *Buddha Fairways* lined with Lotus flowers. I felt very good about what I imagined. As I visualized not just Sam and Charlie, but all the players as bigger Buddhas, I too felt myself becoming an even bigger Buddha.

The first three rounds I played my best golf in years. *Was this a coincidence?* I mused. My attitude and assured ease seemed to create a magnetic effect on my life. As I walked along the range, the other players began doling out compliments such as "Good Playing," "bring it," and "Keep it going."

I thought for sure that because I was leading the event that everyone would be rooting against me. Even Sam Sarazen yelled out "Knock'em dead killer," as we walked towards the 1st tee. Sam's smile appeared genuinely happy for me to succeed.

I remember the Buddha warning me not to get too emotionally high or low over circumstances and to remain detached from outcomes. So, rather than allowing myself to take credit for what seemed like a positive change in Sam specifically, I stood on the 1st tee and began visualizing the fairway as an even brighter, magenta lotus lined *Buddha Fairway*.

Tee shot after tee shot, I was internally calling the mower stripe I was going to land the ball on. Though the first five holes I was wearing my *Buddha Suit,* walking in my *Buddha Fairway,* striking the ball beautifully, I still hadn't knocked in a putt and was still even par. I had yet to hit an iron shot *tap-in* close. I was, however compressing the ball nicely, plus my putter felt right as I gliding along playing each shot with 100% commitment and discipline.

Ward consoled me as he commented, "Remember the *Three Simple Rules to Great Putting*?" "You're hitting your spots *Double A!"* Ward paused, "You have made all your putts. Unfortunately, nothing has gone in the hole so far." Ward continued, "Be patient with yourself. Remember, you stressed to me the importance of managing speed; the ball will eventually drop." Ward continued, "Also, let's not forget we charted the greens, so reading the greens isn't going to be a problem." I was slightly frustrated, I heard my brother's wisdom and took a deep breath nodding in agreement as we huffed our way up the steep hill to the 6th tee.

The 6th hole was beautiful with a well-protected, drivable dogleg right par 4 measuring 288 yards. This short hole was a high-risk, high reward type of hole with a penalty area all along the right side, and bunkers all along the left, which would be a factor during the event. Just before my practice, round Ward and I overheard a couple of members in the locker room laughing as they referred to the 6th hole as "the shortest par 5 north of the Colorado River."

As I stepped onto the tee of this narrow drivable hole, I realized this was my fifth attempt, and I hadn't hit a driver yet. We had played this hole only -1 under par which was conservative considering how straight I can drive the golf ball. As Ward and I studied the yardage book, I began feeling like it was time to play aggressively and get something going.

Grabbing for my TaylorMade M6 Tour driver, I whispered, "This should be perfect if I hit it solid, don't you think?" I asked Ward. "I love that play Double A... Commit to your shot," Ward confirmed.

Going through my normal routine I made a balanced pass at the ball; I looked up just in time to see my shot take off directly at the flag. The distance was spot on as the ball landed on the ground making a loud THWACK, taking a gigantic bounce over the green, the greenside bunker, to what appeared to be Out of Bounds or O.B. into somebody's condo patio.

"Am I imagining things or did that ball just do what I think it did?" I questioned as I looked over at Ward. The bag was already over his shoulder, and my putter was in his hand, ready to trade me clubs. The look of dismay on his face said it all as Ward calmly set the bag on the ground and reached into the bag pulling out a brand-new pellet.

"You may want to hit a provisional ball," Ward suggested as he tossed me a new golf ball.

I walked back to the tee and softly said, "This is a provisional ball; the original ball was a number one; the provisional ball is a number three." I locked onto the pin and hit my second ball onto the green relatively close to the flag.

As I walked closer to the green, I could see my original ball, just as I had suspected the ball was *O.B.* Out of Bounds.

I was speechless, I knew I had just hit a perfect shot, with the perfect distance, and it ended up out of bounds. I giggled as I pictured the interview with Jack Sherpa in my dream with the Buddha.

I recalled Jack's statements, *"When I finally realized that golf is a game of misses, not always about your good shots, rather how well you manage your bad ones."* Jack also expressed, *"Not all good shots end up good, that doesn't make it a bad shot."* This was the perfect example of that mentality.

With zero waves of panic, my provisional ball was now in play as I switched my energy to the next shot. I walked thru the Buddha Fairway and onto the putting surface, directing my energy to the 6' putt for bogey. I marked the ball and tossed it to Ward to be cleaned. I said to myself, *this would definitely feel like a birdie after I make this putt.*

My imaginary *Dakinis* were grooming my *Buddha Suit,* while I crouched behind the ball. I imagined the ball was going into the hole, three times in my mind. As I set up to my ball to putt, I envisioned the ball already in the bottom of the cup. My goal was to go and get the ball out of the hole. With a confident stroke, the ball rolled just like the picture in my head, dead center for bogey. The sound of the ball hitting the bottom of the cup made my heart race with excitement.

This was a momentum saver just like described by Tiger Woods and two points in the *Points Game.*

As I played the final holes of my round, I couldn't help but feel deeper gratitude for my new way of living in the *Buddha Fairway* surrounded by lotus flowers. The warmth in my heart was indescribable as I projected greatness onto everyone in my group, followed by a broadened projection of greatness to the entire field. *Dakinis* began to appear within the gallery that followed along. For the first time in my career, I was experiencing the feeling of weightlessness and freedom from negativity.

It was the most electrifying experience as the positive energy I sent to everyone was bouncing back to me. *Was this golfing ecstasy?* I thought to myself. I continued projecting energy onto my playing partners, and it seemed more putts began to fall, plus the group began to feed off the energy. Everyone in the group played incredibly well in that sublime moment.

I hardly remember thinking of ***how to*** during that final round of golf, as I proceeded up the hill to the 18th tee of the final round. Although the day had been far from perfect, it felt much like driving a car while talking to a friend on the phone. I had used the brake, blinkers, and even changed gears all while talking and never ever thought about ***how to*** drive the car.

I had spent my day interacting with different people and situations like unfortunate bounces, caddies, players, and rules officials all resulting in manifesting the Buddha, *Buddha Fields*, and *Buddha Fairways*.

The feeling of tapping my ball into the hole on the 72nd green was exhilarating. The clapping and whistling of the small gallery heightened my senses and the feeling of satisfaction ran through my body as I thought, *this is almost better than sex!* "This was *golf-gasmic,* to say the least," I revealed to Ward with my enormous smile.

I finally realized this was the final shot of *Tour School* and I hadn't heard a whisper from *Old Andrew* all day.

"Nice job!" Ward yelled as he gave me a huge hug. Charlie and Sam had already pulled off their hats as everyone shook hands. We were in the final pairing as the gallery and the media began flooding onto the green. It was then that I realized thoughts of the score, position, or final outcome hadn't even entered my mind the entire round.

The Three Priceless Techniques had momentarily freed me from attachment, aversion, and delusion and showed me a path to satiation and to my true greatness.

Dream Time

As I dropped Ward off at the airport and he walked away, I saw *Dakinis* surrounding him as he entered the terminal.

Arya and the kids met me at Red Robin our favorite family restaurant to eat, celebrate, and love each other. Everyone was excited to hear about my week, and we traded stories of the day. I barely mentioned my newfound golf future to the children because I knew all they wanted was my love and attention.

Finally, after arriving home, Arya and I caught up on the week's adventures. I explained to her about the Buddha, and how he had armed me with **The Three Priceless Techniques**.

We both smiled as we stared at the congratulatory letter from the **Tour**. As tears began to form in my eyes, I said to Arya, "Thank you for supporting me through the ups and downs of this lifelong journey. This victory wouldn't have been possible without you."

I was ready to hit the sack for the needed rest I was due. I was looking forward to being with the Buddha and reviewing my day.

Sure enough, the Buddha appeared as he had in our previous encounters. He said, "You have much, much more to learn. At this time in your evolution, before receiving more, you are to practice and gain even more proficiency in these **3 PTs,** which will prepare you to receive more."

Yes, I was evolving, and I knew this required time, process, and even mistakes. He said, "There are only two mistakes one can make along the road to truth. Not going all the way and not starting."

"I realized I needed to perfect the **Techniques,"** I told him, "I am committed to going all the way!" For a moment I felt like he was leaving me, but then I realized that he would never do that.

The Buddha had given me so much, and I needed to repay this kindness by applying these **3PTs**. I could swear that I saw him smile at me with approval, and just like that, he was gone...

The Tantric Golf/ Buddha Fields Challenge

Thank you for reading *Tantric Golf, Buddha Fields for Golfers*! We hope you enjoyed the story!

Are you up for a challenge? While you might have trepidation about applying **The Three Priceless Techniques**, or if they will work for you, we (dare) challenge you to take the **Buddha Fields Challenge!**

It is said that it takes twenty-one days to create a habit. The **Buddha Fields Challenge** is a commitment to practice **The Three Priceless Techniques** for the next 21 days. Put them to the test and see how you feel; watch how you progress on your own Buddha-Scale and how much your world improves.

It's a good idea to read this book at least once a week during this period. With each read, you'll glean new levels of understanding, have even more experiences and enjoy new revelations.

Our goal is to inspire seven million people to do **The Three Priceless Techniques** consistently. Please let us know that you are committing with us to this Challenge and email us at BuddhaFieldsChallenge@gmail.com We are here to support you in creating global **Buddha Fields Meditation Groups.**

To further help you improve your world and the world at large, we recommend you do the **Buddha Fields Meditation** daily. This twenty-two-minute meditation will accelerate your Buddha Nature and help the world to do the same. It is available to download at www.buddhafields.org for only $9. The **Buddha Fields Healing Sanctuary Meditation** is also available if you need extra help healing your physical, emotional, and mental bodies.

Reviews are priceless! Sharing is caring. If you deemed this book valuable, please share your thoughts in an **Amazon** Review.

Again, thank you for reading this book. We believe that a picture is worth a thousand words, and an experience is worth a million. Rather than sharing what you learned in the book, it is best to let others have their own experience and recommend the book be read.

We hope to meet you in the Buddha Field!

Love and Tujechey*

Daniel O'Hara and Kevin PomArleau

*(Is Tibetan for may you achieve enlightenment in this incarnation.)

Dedications/Acknowledgements

Special thanks to... (from Kevin)

Daniel O'Hara for giving me the opportunity to co-author, *Tantric Golf- Buddha Fields for Golfers*. Meeting Daniel at a Tony Robbins function in L.A. was definitely divine intervention.

My incredible parents, Terry and Nani PomArleau who allowed me every opportunity possible to have and live a blessed life.

My brother Heath PomArleau for his fierce competition and for driving me to become a better player. I really loved kicking your ass when we were kids, and through all things, we are blood, you are the best brother ever.

Stephanie Granik, the love of my life and her three beautiful children Caitlyn, Kayla and Brayden for keeping me young and driven to succeed.

My oldest daughter Demi Mai, her husband Jacinth and my two grandsons Kairon and Raiden. I love you all.

My youngest Daughter Jaice Rai and husband Josh for re-entering my life and teaching me it's never too late.

Peyton Ross who continues to work hard. Keep driving towards your dreams.

Hypnotist Gina *Magic* Coffman for introducing me to a different way of thinking while playing the game I so dearly cherish and love.

Dr. Tom Iwashita for your knowledge of the body.

Dr. Craig Farnsworth your endless putting knowledge.

Special thanks to… (from Daniel)

To my most amazing co-author Kevin, or should I say *Double A*, PomArleau. You outdid yourself! It is a Hole-In-One from 180 yards out!

To my dear father, T. Patrick O'Hara, who loved the game of golf, who I dearly wish could've had the opportunity to enjoy this wonderful book. I hope I made you proud! I miss you and love you!

To Master Choa, who taught me and empowered me in every area of my life. Thank you!

Gina "Magic" Coffman of www.ResetGolf.com, your "Magic" is truly magical! Your gifts of compassion and consciousness in helping people are off the charts!

Dr. Tom Iwashita of www.theAthletesAdvantage.com, my close friend of nearly 40 years. I'm so proud of your being the Olympic Team Dr and am grateful you rehabbed my knee without surgery. After my knee collapsed, moving inward more than six inches, and while every other doctor would have wanted to operate--you healed it without surgery. You and your team are world class.

Karan Vir and www.VimanikaComics.com you guys rock! Thank you for your patience and persistence for creating our beautiful cover.

Mr. Peters aka Tom Peters (now that I'm an adult), was my favorite teacher in high school. He even gave me a copy of the book *Siddhartha.* Thank you for your inspiration and editing help.

Thank you, Parie Petty, at www.WesternLithographics.com for again coalescing our cover.

About the Authors

Kevin A. PomArleau was born in the summer of 69' in Sunnymead, California and grew up in Wenatchee, Washington. He fell in love with the game of golf at the age of eight and began playing competitively at the age of 12. After two years of college, he joined the military and served for seven years as an Air Traffic Control (ATC) specialist in the USAF. Spending several years in Japan, he adopted Buddhism in pursuit of a happier life and potentially a better golf game. After leaving the ATC job and becoming a professional golfer, he has spent more than 22 years seeking golf and life enlightenment.

Daniel O'Hara learned the game of golf from his late father, Theodore "Pat" O'Hara (Jan. 2, 1926 to Jan. 2, 2010), who taught him how to swing a club in their backyard and about the old-time greats like Slammin' Sammy Snead. At the age of 12, Daniel developed a passion for the martial arts that turned into a long-term love affair that he later combined with the meditative arts. He met his "Buddha" who was a real-life Yoda in '94, and he taught Daniel about energy and spiritual development. He has consulted with and has been endorsed by numerous professional athletes from the NFL, NBA, MLB, UFC and more. At 30, Daniel was featured on a major radio show in L.A. in which he touched a woman on the back of her neck and in under four minutes gave her an orgasm. He is the lead author of three book franchises: *Buddha Fields, Christ's Castle, and Krishna's Kingdom.* As a philanthropist, he is committed to helping as many people as possible get out of suffering. You can learn more about him at www.DanielOHara.com.

Products/Services Endorsed in *Tantric Golf*

www.Flexputter.com Use code Tantric for a discount

www.Filtersteve.com If you want to breath clean air

www.Mamatspetproducts.com

www.BlackcloverUSA.com- Living Lucky Hats

www.Francisedward.com

www.theAthletesAdvantage.com- Dr. Tom Iwashita

www.ResetGolf.com- Gina *Magic* Sports Hypnosis and Performance Enhancement

www.JNHLifestyles.com- Best infrared saunas (with NO EMF)

www.NickDelgado.com- One of the top Anti-Aging Docs & World Record Holder for Strength & Endurance

Made in the USA
San Bernardino, CA
07 March 2020